His eyes darkened as his gaze leveled with hers. "I just want you safe. It's what I've wanted from the beginning of this whole mess."

Her heart contracted. "Scanlon—"

His head dipped. For a second, she was certain he was going to kiss her. But he froze in place, his gaze falling to rest on her parted lips. "Damn it, Cooper—"

It was a familiar point in time, she realized. A point of no return, when the tension buzzing between them could take on a new and dangerous tenor. They'd reached this point before, during long and harrowing cases when the whole world seemed to be spinning out of control. Moments when a little human connection provided a temptation almost too exquisite to resist.

But one of them always moved. Always backed away before they did something that couldn't be undone. She waited for the inevitable retreat, for Scanlon to pull away and rise to his feet, putting distance and cold air between them.

That moment never came.

PAULA GRAVES

SECRET HIDEOUT

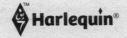

Harlequin®

TORONTO NEW YORK LONDON
AMSTERDAM PARIS SYDNEY HAMBURG
STOCKHOLM ATHENS TOKYO MILAN MADRID
PRAGUE WARSAW BUDAPEST AUCKLAND

For Jenn, my critique partner, who keeps me honest and keeps me writing. Thanks for everything you do.

Recycling programs
for this product may
not exist in your area.

ISBN-13: 978-0-373-74663-7

SECRET HIDEOUT

Copyright © 2012 by Paula Graves

Printed in U.S.A.

ABOUT THE AUTHOR

Alabama native Paula Graves wrote her first book, a mystery starring herself and her neighborhood friends, at the age of six. A voracious reader, Paula loves books that pair tantalizing mystery with compelling romance. When she's not reading or writing, she works as a creative director for a Birmingham advertising agency and spends time with her family and friends. She is a member of Southern Magic Romance Writers, Heart of Dixie Romance Writers and Romance Writers of America.

Paula invites readers to visit her website, www.paulagraves.com.

Books by Paula Gravess

HARLEQUIN INTRIGUE
926—FORBIDDEN TERRITORY
998—FORBIDDEN TEMPTATION
1046—FORBIDDEN TOUCH
1088—COWBOY ALIBI
1183—CASE FILE: CANYON CREEK, WYOMING*
1189—CHICKASAW COUNTY CAPTIVE*
1224—ONE TOUGH MARINE*
1230—BACHELOR SHERIFF*
1272—HITCHED AND HUNTED**
1278—THE MAN FROM GOSSAMER RIDGE**
1285—COOPER VENGEANCE**
1305—MAJOR NANNY
1337—SECRET IDENTITY‡
1342—SECRET HIDEOUT‡

*Cooper Justice
**Cooper Justice: Cold Case Investigation
‡Cooper Security

CAST OF CHARACTERS

Isabel Cooper—Ambushed and drugged by masked men in the hotel where she's staying, the former FBI agent gets away with the help of her dead partner's ghost. But when she wakes to find him very much alive, how far will she go to help the man who deceived her into believing he was dead?

Ben Scanlon—The bomb meant for his partner came close to killing him instead. When his boss gave him the chance to "die" in order to go undercover to find the backwoods bomber who targeted his partner, he took it. Will the investigation also answer his lingering questions about his father's death?

Adam Brand—The FBI Special Agent in Charge let Isabel believe her partner died. Does he have a hidden agenda now that he wants them working together again?

Addie Tolliver—The middle-aged store owner is the head of the Swain crime family now that her brother Jasper is doing life in jail. Is she as wily as her brother, or could she be the weak link that could help topple the whole family?

J. T. Swain—The mysterious new Swain seems to have links to a band of crooked mercenaries who have given Isabel's family trouble before. Is the Swain family business looking to expand their criminal enterprise?

Dahlia McCoy—Despite Scanlon's attempt to court her to take advantage of her brother's connection to the Swains, the pretty accountant seems to be squeaky clean. But is there more to Dahlia than Scanlon thinks?

Opal Butler—Jasper Swain's other sister has never shown any interest in the family business. So why is she back in town and what is her agenda?

Chapter One

The man down the hall was definitely watching her. And given how grubby she looked at the moment, Isabel Cooper didn't think he was ogling her for the usual reasons.

Reaching for the handle of the ice machine door, she dropped her room key card on purpose, giving herself an excuse to shift position and sneak a better look at the man lurking at the end of the hall. He was lean and sandy-haired, wearing a simple black T-shirt and faded jeans. As her gaze rose toward him, he looked away. But she was certain he'd been staring.

Hair prickling on the back of her neck, she scooped ice into her bucket and headed back to her room. The carpeted hallway muffled even her own footsteps, so she couldn't hear anyone moving up the hallway behind her.

But she could feel him.

Even though her room was straight ahead, she hooked a quick left into the elevator alcove. It was a dead end, but it gave her a chance to set herself for a fight.

She waited, her breath burning in her lungs.

But no one appeared around the corner.

The elevator dinged behind her, making her jump. The couple emerging from the elevator gave her a curious look. In the mirrored back of the open elevator, she caught a glimpse of her reflection, a wild-eyed brunette in a T-shirt and yoga pants, her feet stuck in a pair of fleece-lined house shoes and her unruly curls caught up in a lopsided ponytail.

The couple turned left, toward her own hotel room. She followed, darting a quick look down the hallway where she'd seen the loitering man. The corridor was empty.

Isabel released a puff of air. Wasn't it time to stop looking for criminals around every corner? Six months had already passed since she'd resigned from the FBI and returned home to work for her brother.

Six months since she'd buried her partner and said her final goodbye to the man she'd worked with for years, since she was a snot-nosed green agent fresh out of Quantico.

God, she missed him.

Trudging to her hotel room, she pushed the painful thoughts of Scanlon from her mind, thinking about the man she'd seen in the hallway instead. He hadn't looked familiar. And apparently she'd only imagined that he'd shadowed her up the hallway.

Tucking the ice bucket under one arm, she swiped the key card in the lock and let herself inside the hotel room. The door clicked shut, engaging the automatic lock. On instinct, she engaged the safety lock as well, waiting for the prickling sensation on the back of her neck to subside. But it lingered, the tingle of a thousand spider legs dancing across her skin.

She darted to the mirrored dresser, put down the ice bucket next to her overnight case and unzipped the bag, feeling inside for her Beretta 9 mm. She shouldn't have left the room without her weapon, but there was nowhere she could hide it in her yoga pants, and she hadn't wanted to alarm the other hotel visitors.

She ran her hands around the inside of her bag one more time, her fingers moving frantically in search of the weapon.

It wasn't there.

Her heart lurched into higher gear, pounding against her breastbone, as she picked up the bag to see if it could have fallen out without her noticing.

As she moved, her gaze glanced across the mirror on the wall above the dresser. Her heart jolted as she saw a man in a black ski mask standing a few inches behind her, holding her Beretta in his gloved hand.

Terror sucked the breath from her lungs.

"Looking for this?" The man behind the mask spoke in a low, pronounced drawl, the unabashed rural accent of the north Alabama hills.

"You can take all my money," she said, careful to sound neither too weak nor too strong. "Take the gun, too. I won't give you any trouble."

The man laughed. "Turn around."

She obeyed, sucking in another quick breath when she realized the man was not alone. A second man, similarly masked and clad in a dark long-sleeved T-shirt and pants, stood nearby, watching her. He didn't seem to be armed but was large enough, muscular enough, to pose a problem if she had to fight her way out of the situation.

The adrenaline coursing through her veins screamed for her to run. Catch them by surprise. But she'd engaged the safety lock—she'd never get it open in time to make her escape.

Was that the point of the man down the hall? To spook her into taking the extra precaution?

Think, Cooper. How do you get out of this?

"What do you want?" she asked, her voice strained.

"You don't know?" The man sounded surprised.

"You don't want money?" she asked, though it was clear her assailants weren't here for anything as ordinary as robbery.

"Agent Cooper, you're too smart to play games with us."

Which answered one question, she thought. They knew who she was. Their agenda was personal, not random.

But why? She wasn't working a case of any sort— she was here in Fort Payne, Alabama, to give a talk to some mystery writers about investigative procedure. It had been months since she'd worked any cases for the FBI, and she wasn't even working an open case with Cooper Security at the moment.

What would bring three armed men to her hotel room?

"I don't know what you want from me," she said aloud.

The man holding the gun on her glanced toward the other man. Isabel took advantage of his brief inattention and grabbed the ice bucket off the dresser, swinging it at his gun hand. The Beretta went flying, smacking against the motel room wall.

She ran to the door, her fingers clawing at the safety latch. As it flipped open, hands circled her throat and gave a backward jerk. She choked as her windpipe began to close from the pressure, black spots forming in her vision.

"Do it now!" her captor growled, dragging her onto the bed. Terror eclipsed the sense of suffocation as she struggled against the hands holding her down. The pressure on her throat eased, and she sucked in a lungful of air. Her vision returned in time to see a flash of a needle descending toward her neck.

She screamed for help, fighting harder. The man who'd had her gun shoved his gloved hand against her mouth, laughing as she bit at the leather. "Scream again, and we'll kill you now."

The needle descended, pricking the side of her neck.

The men held her in place, laughing at her struggles, until she felt her lungs burning for air. The room began to spin and grow strangely out of proportion. On the wall, the bland painting of daffodils started to melt, the colors sliding down the wall to pool atop the dresser.

One of the men had moved away from her, she realized, wondering how that could be possible when it seemed as if a dozen pair of hands still held her down.

She felt powerless to move against the pressure keeping her immobile. Forcing her gaze upward, she found herself staring into a pair of piercing blue eyes.

Jasper Swain, she thought, giving a start when she realized the words had escaped her aching throat in a rasp.

The blue eyes widened.

Then they bled.

And she screamed.

THE CRY DIED QUICKLY, but he knew what he'd heard. It was her. And she wasn't alone.

He flattened himself against the wall of the ice maker alcove down the hall from her room, knowing how disastrous it would be if one of the men inside caught sight of him. But he couldn't let them take her out of here.

He'd considered calling in a tip to the police, but the men in that room were dangerous, reckless men who'd have little compunction about leaving a small-town cop bleeding out in a hotel corridor. The cops would be more likely to get in his way than help him get her to safety.

He closed his fingers around the Glock hidden in the pocket of his windbreaker, grimacing. He wasn't the world's best marksman himself. But unlike local law enforcement officers, at least he knew what he was up against from the start.

How in hell did they think they were going to get her out of here? Was that even the plan anymore? He'd been damned lucky to hear about what the Swains were planning in the first place, considering how close-mouthed the people of Bolen Bluff, Alabama, could be.

He'd overheard the conversation while snooping around Tolliver Feed and Seed. Hidden in the back room, he'd eavesdropped on two Swain clansmen talking cryptically about an operation the next day, something to do with a woman at a Fort Payne hotel.

And if the Swains were up to something, it was bad news.

Down the hall, a door opened, and he heard scuffling sounds. He forced himself to remain in place as footsteps thudded down the hall toward his position.

He edged toward the ice machine, tugging the bill of his baseball cap lower over his face. He didn't have an ice bucket, but someone had helpfully left spares stacked on top of the machine, so he grabbed one of those and opened the ice machine bin. As he dug into the ice, he heard footsteps shuffling past him at a quick clip.

Once they'd passed, he took a quick look down the hall after them. He caught sight of a mass of dark curls and his heart gave a disconcerting flip.

Two men flanked her, holding her up as she sagged against them. A third man lagged behind, watching their backs. All of them wore caps low over their faces, just like his.

They were heading for the stairs.

He waited for them to enter the stairwell before he hurried after them. Cracking the door open, he listened for a second, trying to gauge how far ahead they were.

The footsteps echoed in the cavernous stairwell, making it hard to be sure where the sounds were coming from. He slipped into the stairwell and eased after them, keeping close to the wall to stay out of sight.

He had no idea how he was going to get her away from them without being seen, but if it came to a choice, he'd risk identification to save her. Whatever it took, he was going to get Isabel Cooper away from her captors.

What happened after that, however, would be anyone's guess.

SHE WAS IN A CAVERN. A tall, twisting cavern, painted in hieroglyphics that almost seemed like words.

Almost.

The almost-words shimmered on the walls as if they were painted with glitter. Sometimes they slid down the walls and slid back up again, making her dizzy.

And still she and her captors descended. Down, down, down, into the pits of hell.

Jasper Swain's eyes had stopped bleeding. At least, she thought they had. He'd taken off the mask, but his cap bill was so low that all she could see of his face was a deep shadow.

And she knew he wasn't Jasper Swain, either. Swain was still in prison in St. Clair County, not due for his next parole hearing for at least five more years. Her head was playing games with her.

She remembered a needle. They'd shot her full of something. Something potent. That was why the walls were melting and she was seeing people who weren't there.

"What do you want with me?" she asked, raising her head to look at the one she still thought of as Swain.

He didn't answer, and his shadowy face seemed to undulate in front of her eyes. She dragged her gaze away from the mesmerizing dance and gazed upward, wondering if someone had heard her screams.

What she saw on the landing above nearly made her racing heart stop in its tracks.

She was seeing another person who wasn't there.

Couldn't be there.

The face was almost as familiar to her now as her own reflection in the mirror. Maybe even more familiar, considering how much she'd seemed to change over the last six months. He'd changed little at all. A little more scruffy, as if her hallucinating mind had conjured up the beard stubble she'd secretly wanted to see on his clean-shaven jaw. His hair was longer, too, no longer combed back into a neatly groomed cut that seemed to scream "federal agent."

Oh, Scanlon, she thought, blinking back sudden tears when his ghost disappeared from sight. A fresh sense of loss overwhelmed her, oddly energizing. Rage infused her—rage at her own sense of powerlessness, at the ravening grief slowly eating her from the inside out.

He's gone. He's not coming back. And you'll be gone, too, if you don't get your head back together and figure out how to get away from these goons.

The walls around her closed in, threatening to trigger claustrophobia. Seeing what she thought was an exit door on the next stair landing, she focused hard, making out the number two. Second floor.

She knew the first-floor door opened onto a narrow corridor from which a person could either head down the hall to the front lobby or go out a side door to the parking lot. She'd gone that route earlier that morning, when a couple of the conference coordinators had taken her out for breakfast.

If they got her to the first floor, they'd be out to the parking lot before her screams could grab anyone's attention.

She tensed her muscles and glanced upward again, hoping to see Scanlon's ghost. But he didn't make a reappearance. She tamped down a rush of sorrow.

Now, she thought.

She let herself sag heavily against the two men holding her upright. The sudden shift in weight caught them by surprise, giving her an opening.

Swinging as hard as she could, she jabbed her elbows into their crotches and pushed to her feet, jerking free as they reacted to the pain of her blows.

The door to the second floor was right in front of her, shimmering and undulating. She pushed through it, ignoring the ruckus behind her.

"Get her," she heard one man say, his voice a pained croak.

She didn't look back, racing down a writhing, spinning tunnel. There was still enough sense left in her drugged-out brain to realize she was running down the second-floor hallway of the hotel. She gave a half second's thought to banging on the doors, looking for help, but she suspected the people inside those rooms, even if they answered her knocks, would see her swaying and drunk-eyed and slam the door in her face.

Worse, the men she heard pounding down the hall behind her might kill anyone who answered.

She found her strength flagging, and even though she had put a fair amount of space between herself and the men running behind her, she knew they must be gaining.

She had blown past the elevators, knowing she couldn't risk waiting for one to arrive, but there was a second set of stairs at the end of the corridor that led down to the parking lot. It was on the opposite side of the hotel from where she'd parked her little green Ford Mustang, but at least she'd be outside with more room to maneuver.

She hit the door to the stairwell at a dead run, stumbling into the railing and nearly pitching head-first down the stairs.

She heard footsteps pounding from above her, coming down a flight of stairs at a clip. Had one of them circled back, anticipating her destination?

She started running down the steps, but whatever they had injected into her neck was hitting its stride, making her head swim as if she'd just spent the last ten minutes riding a tilt-a-whirl. She stumbled a few steps above the landing and pitched forward, landing hard.

The air whooshed from her lungs, making her vision go black. As she struggled to breathe again, she heard a thudding of footsteps racing down to where she lay.

She tried to push to her feet, but she didn't have the strength. She felt a pair of strong, warm hands drag her to her feet. She blinked, trying to make sense of what she was seeing.

The ghost of Ben Scanlon stared back at her, his blue eyes soft and so beautifully familiar that tears filmed over her eyes, blurring his features.

"Scanlon," she whispered.

"No time, sugar," he answered in Scanlon's voice, the cocky Texas twang she'd first hated, then grown to love.

But he was dead. She'd seen the aftermath of the explosion. Examined the autopsy report. Watched his casket lowered into a grave in the tiny town of Maribel, Texas. Held his mama's hand as she'd cried.

She was hallucinating. One of her captors had found her and grabbed her again. That was all it could be.

But she didn't have the strength to fight anymore. The appearance of Scanlon's ghost seemed like a mercy, one last chance to be with her partner again before she met whatever fate her captors had planned for her.

Giving in to the fantasy, she stopped resisting and let Scanlon's ghost lead her quickly down the stairs and out into the blinding sunlight.

He slipped a jacket over her shoulders as they reached the side of a dark green van. Dragging her around until her back met the solid wall of the panel van, he pulled the cap off his own head and shoved it onto hers.

She blinked with confusion, opening her mouth to ask what he was doing. A strange halo limned his body, an aura of brilliant blues and dazzling greens. She'd never seen anything so beautiful in her life.

His hands cradled her face, his touch crackling like electricity. His bent head blocked out the sunlight as he touched his mouth to hers.

Fire flowed from his lips into hers, poured through her veins in a flood of bright sensation, immolating her from the inside out.

She wound her arms around his neck and pressed closer until she melted into him, their bodies melding until she no longer existed outside of him. A low groan rumbled through her. She didn't know which of them had made the sound.

The world disappeared into a brilliant pinpoint of light, pulsating with colors that throbbed and danced until they finally exploded like supernova.

The fireworks fell away, fading into a cold, black void, and it was a long time before Isabel formed a conscious thought again.

Chapter Two

Consciousness returned in sickening waves, crashing against a wall of agony in her head. Even the small effort of opening her eyes seemed beyond Isabel's strength, so she suffered awhile longer in a dark cocoon, willing the nausea to subside.

Where was she? Why so much pain? Why had she been asleep?

Movement nearby forced her to open her eyes. Wincing as light needled into her brain, she bit back a moan and focused on a man standing with his back to her as he stirred something in a battered pot on an old gas range.

Scanlon, she thought, even though she knew it couldn't be so.

Then he turned to grab a spice tin from the counter beside the range, making her gasp. The aquiline nose and stubborn chin definitely belonged to her former FBI partner.

Her *dead* partner.

He turned around at her gasp, his blue eyes soft. "Hey there, Cooper. Back among the living?"

She shook her head, seized by fear. Had she lost her mind? Was that why she couldn't remember where she was or why she was here? "You're dead."

"Cooper—"

"No, you died! Six months ago! I saw footage of the explosion. I—I read the autopsy report." She swiped tears from her cheeks with a jerk of her hand. "I held your mama's hand as we buried you—"

Pain flickered across his expression. "I know."

"I don't believe in ghosts!" If she wasn't dreaming, then she was crazy. Loss could do that, and she'd been hiding her own grief all this time, trying not to worry her family or even admit to herself how important Scanlon had been to her—

"I'm not a ghost." He crouched beside her, threading his solid fingers between her own. The warmth from his hands worked its way up her arm into her chest. Hot tears burned her eyes and she let them fall, staring at him in disbelief. She reached up to touch his stubbled jaw, wondering if her hand would slide right through him. But he was solid. Warm.

Alive.

He caught her face between his hands and made her look into his eyes. "I know it's confusing, but I'm here. I didn't die in the explosion. I was there, but I escaped."

An ache settled in the center of her chest. "But you let me think you were dead." The buoyant happiness that had kept her upright for the past few seconds fled as suddenly as it had arrived, supplanted by a rush of anger. She pushed against him. "You were alive and you let me think you were dead!"

"It's complicated—"

"How could you do that to me? We were partners! You don't do that to your partner!" Growling, she tried to throw off the patchwork quilt tangled around her legs, but the pain in her head grew excruciating. She jammed the heels of her hands into her temples, certain her head was going to explode.

The bed beneath her shifted, making the world roil around her again. Scanlon's hands closed around her upper arms, steadying her. "You have to calm down. You're still suffering the effects of whatever they gave you."

An image darted through her brain. A flash of light on the point of a needle. A corresponding sting pricked the side of her neck. The alarming memory did more to dispel her escalating rage than anything Scanlon could have said.

"Somebody shot me up with something."

"I know. There's a needle mark near your carotid, and you were hallucinating before you passed out." His voice emerged as hard as steel. "Stupid cretins could have killed you."

"Who?" Why couldn't she remember anything more than the needle? It felt as if she'd walked into a solid wall, nothing but blankness wherever she looked. "Who did this to me?"

"I'm not sure." He dropped his hands from her

arms and averted his gaze. She realized he wasn't telling her the truth.

But why?

She changed tacks. "Any idea what they shot me up with?"

"Not sure about that, either." He stood and crossed to the saucepan on the stove. "Food will help, whatever it was. Dilute the effects, at least."

She wasn't sure her rolling stomach could handle a glass of water, much less whatever it was he was pouring from the saucepan into a bowl. As he pulled a sleeve of plain crackers from a nearby cabinet, he asked, "You want to eat in bed or do you feel like sitting up at the table?"

"I don't know if I can hold anything down."

"Give it a try, at least." He brought the bowl of steaming liquid to the bed, which she now realized was actually a futon sofa that took up half the wall in the small room. The rest of the room was cramped by the furnishings—a stove, a sink and a refrigerator, plus a card table that seemed to serve as a dining table, sat across from her. A door, the futon and a small bookshelf took up the wall behind her. The narrow end wall was just large enough to accommodate a low table with a television set that looked decades old.

"Where are we?" she asked.

He placed the bowl of soup on a portable tray table pulled from the narrow space between the stove and the refrigerator. "Soup first. I'll tell you everything in a minute, I promise."

She eyed the bowl, a little freaked out at being suspicious of Ben Scanlon. "What *is* that?"

"Chicken noodle soup." He set the tray table in front of her. Up close, she noticed for the first time a wicked-looking scar on the back of his left hand.

He saw her reaction. "I didn't escape the bomb entirely." He turned his hand over, palm up, and she saw that the scar extended to his palm as well. "A piece of bomb shrapnel went straight through my hand. Hurt like hell."

Any hint of appetite fled. "Any other injuries?"

"Scrapes and cuts. I got knocked into the river by the blast. Lost consciousness and damned near drowned before I came to and coughed up the water I'd inhaled."

"They said they identified your body—" She shuddered, the memory of that day flooding back with fresh sharpness.

"Brand arranged it."

She stared at him. "Adam Brand knew you were alive the whole time?" The SAC—Special Agent in Charge—had been one of the few people who'd seemed to understand her difficulty in dealing with Scanlon's murder. Brand knew she'd felt guilty when she learned her partner had intercepted a note meant for her and gotten killed trying to protect her. He'd even understood her choice to leave the FBI.

So he wouldn't have to lie to her face every day?

"We couldn't let anyone connect me to what I'm doing here." Scanlon slanted a guilty look at her. "Even you."

Especially me, she thought blackly. "Where is here?"

"First, let's get a little chicken noodle soup into you before you keel over on me."

"Not until you tell me what the hell's going on." She pressed her lips together.

Scanlon sighed. "Where do you want me to start?"

"The explosion," she said flatly. "That message was left on my desk. Morelli told me that much. You took *my* message from Morelli and met with *my* informant. Why would you do that? Why wouldn't you call me, at least?"

Scanlon's scarred hand stretched toward her for a second before dropping back to his lap. "I thought it was a setup."

"So you went in my place? Without any backup?"

"Brand was with me, watching in case anything went hinky."

She tamped down her simmering anger, trying to be dispassionate. "Did you trigger a booby trap?" That was the finding after an exhaustive postmortem of the explosion. But now she wondered if anything Brand had told her was the truth.

"It was on a delay—meant to give me time to get all the way inside before it blew. But I saw—something—" He frowned, as if making a mental effort to return to that moment in time. "I had a concussion from the blast. It seems to have erased my memories of what happened when I stepped inside the warehouse."

"Then how do you know you spotted something?"

Scanlon's mouth curved slightly. "I was wired for sound, at least until I ended up in the river. Brand told me I said something about a trap and then all of a sudden I was hauling butt away from the place."

The temperature in the room seemed to drop a few degrees as Isabel pictured, not for the first time, what those last few seconds before the blast must have felt like for him. At least, this time, she could add a happier ending.

If he's telling the truth, a bleak voice in the back of her head added.

She needed to talk to Brand. She had trouble believing he'd known this whole time. He had been so supportive—

"I quit the FBI within two weeks, you know," she said aloud. "It was hard enough to go into that office every day and see your empty desk. When they brought in a new agent—"

"I know. Brand told me." Scanlon leaned toward her, his expression troubled. "Go back to the Bureau. Brand will take you back—I know he will. As soon as we get you out of here."

The last thing she wanted was to go back to the FBI, especially if Scanlon was telling her the truth.

The idea that people she believed she could trust would lie to her this way…

She felt completely betrayed.

"I'm working with my brother now," she said aloud. "At the security company. We're doing good things there."

"I thought you weren't happy about your brother's security company when he first came up with the idea."

She hadn't been thrilled. Her experiences with private security firms while working for the FBI had been more negative than positive. But Jesse's concept for the security firm appealed to her. The big jobs they undertook financed the low-cost and pro bono cases Cooper Security chose on an individual, need-by-need basis.

"Things have changed," she admitted.

Scanlon's eyes narrowed. "I guess they have." He waved at the bowl of soup. "At least have a bite or two. It'll help your body fight off the effects of what they gave you."

She forced herself to eat a few bites of the soup, knowing Scanlon had a stubborn streak that was nearly impossible to thwart. If she wanted answers, she'd have to play along with his rules, even if a bowl of chicken noodle soup was the last thing she wanted at the moment.

But she managed to finish half the bowl and even nibble on a couple of crackers by the time Scanlon had poured the rest of the soup into a plastic container and put it in the small refrigerator next to the stove.

She had so many questions racing through her mind, she felt overwhelmed, especially since the food had done nothing to ease her raging headache. She couldn't think with her pulse pounding in her ears. The lights inside were dimmed, and heavy curtains shut out whatever light might be coming from outside the windows, but her eyes still ached from the glare.

"I need to go to the bathroom," she said. To her alarm, the words came out slurred.

Scanlon crossed quickly to the futon and helped her up. Tugging her hand away from his when he showed every sign of walking with her to the bathroom, she said, "I can handle this myself. Just point me in the right direction."

He stared back at her, his expression hard to read.

Unease fluttered in her stomach. "Please don't tell me the bathroom's outdoors."

His expression cleared. "No. Through that door, take a right down the hall and it's the first door on the left."

She followed his directions and entered the tiny bathroom. It had a toilet and an ancient pedestal sink on one side of the room, and an even more ancient claw-foot tub on the other. She looked longingly at the tub, tempted by the thought of a nice, hot bath, but settled for running cold water in the sink and splashing it on her hot face.

As she was about to head back to the front room, her gaze caught on the window next to the toilet. It was closed off by thick green curtains. She eased the curtains open and took a peek outside, squinting as bright daylight assaulted her eyes.

There were woods outside, dense with new growth. The house seemed to have very little in the way of a yard.

Movement outside caught her eye. A man, she realized. His dark green baseball cap came into view first, dipped forward as the wearer looked down, watching his footing.

Instinctively, she narrowed the opening in the curtains to a crack. As he emerged into the clearing behind the house, the man in the cap looked up, directly toward the window.

Her heart gave a little flop.

She'd seen him before.

He wore a black T-shirt under a faded denim jacket. His jeans were equally faded. His sandy hair curled lightly around the edge of the cap.

Where had she seen him before? She could picture him in her mind, sandy hair, black T-shirt, faded jeans—

No cap. He hadn't been wearing a cap. Not then.

The door behind her opened, making her whirl around in alarm. The sudden movement made her vision swim, and she had to grab the sink to keep from toppling over.

Scanlon rushed in, cupping her elbow to steady

her. "Go to my bedroom. Now. Hide in the closet. No time to explain—"

"There's a man outside. I know I've seen him before—"

"There's more than one man outside," Scanlon said tersely, leading her across the hall to a small, spare bedroom. He opened the door next to the bed to reveal a tiny closet and nudged her inside. "Just stay here and be quiet, no matter what you hear. Promise me."

She nodded. "Are you in danger?"

He brushed her cheek with his fingertips. "I'm always in danger these days, Cooper." He closed the door, plunging the cramped closet into darkness.

BEN SCANLON RECOVERED HIS calm as he walked to the front room. Already, Davy McCoy was banging on the door, commencing the visit Scanlon had been expecting since he'd grabbed Isabel Cooper at the Fort Payne hotel and rushed her out to the van the FBI resident agency in Huntsville had supplied. He hadn't gotten a good look at any of the men, but he knew Davy was involved. Davy was the one he'd overheard making plans for the ambush.

He swept a final glance around the living room, making sure he'd left no signs of Isabel's presence. She'd slipped on her shoes before she'd gone to the bathroom, and he'd already returned the futon to its sofa position.

He took a deep breath and opened the door.

Davy McCoy was a short, wiry man in his mid-twenties, with dark hair thinning prematurely and a sneering smile that was a permanent fixture on his vulpine face. He didn't wait to be asked in, pushing past Scanlon and entering the living room.

"You cookin' somethin'?" He sniffed the air.

"Just soup."

Davy eyed the bowl in the sink. "Been out today?"

The van Scanlon had driven to the hotel was hidden in an abandoned barn a half mile down the mountain, where he'd left his battered old Ford pickup while he was in Fort Payne. But he and Isabel hadn't been back long. If Davy had touched the hood of the Ford, would it still be warm?

"Drove over to Silorville Pond to see if the blue-gills were bedding," he answered, the lie effortless. Lying came all too easy to him these days. "No luck."

"Little early yet, I guess."

Scanlon knew Davy didn't have a particular reason to suspect he'd been involved in thwarting the attempted abduction. Nobody among Bolen Bluff's tight-knit community of weed growers and meth mechanics knew what he'd overheard that night at the feed store. He'd made damned sure he wasn't seen.

But he'd been in Bolen Bluff only a few months. Strangers were automatically suspect. The paranoia among the Swain clan was legendary. One wrong move could get a man killed.

Scanlon knew that better than anyone.

Davy was clearly searching the room with his gaze. He didn't even bother to hide it. "Mind if I use your bathroom?"

Scanlon nodded toward the hallway, hoping the rapid thump of his pulse wasn't audible. It swished so loudly in his ears he barely heard Davy's footsteps as he clomped down the hall.

He went to close the front door that Davy had left open and spotted Bobby Rawlings standing out in the yard, watching him through narrowed eyes. Rawlings was even scarier than McCoy in some ways. He was a Swain by blood, son of one of old Jasper's cousins. That gave him even more carte blanche for violence around these parts than Davy, who was only a Swain clan member out of criminal loyalty.

He gave Rawlings a wave. Rawlings didn't wave back. Scanlon hadn't expected he would.

He closed the door and turned as Davy's heavy bootfalls heralded his return. "You and Bobby been out hunting coyote this morning?"

"Yeah," Davy answered flatly.

"Any luck?"

"Got close, once. Just missed the bitch." Davy shrugged. "We'll find her again. Next time, ain't gonna mess around—just put a bullet straight in her brain."

Scanlon's blood chilled.

"Thanks for the use of your facilities." Davy

slanted a look at Scanlon. "Reckon you'll be comin' to town Saturday?"

"I can," he said carefully, not sure where Davy was going with the question.

"Addie Tolliver's throwin' a barbecue Saturday afternoon for Leamon's birthday."

Addie Tolliver was one of the Swain sisters. She and her son Leamon ran the feed shop in town, and he was pretty sure that Addie was the main mover and shaker in the Swain family's meth and weed business. The family often used the store's back room as a meeting place. He also suspected that the storage area may have been a temporary holding area for drug shipments going out to other parts of the state, though the one time he'd been able to sneak into the back room, all he'd accomplished was overhearing the plan to go after Isabel.

"The Brubakers are comin' over from Higdon to play," Davy continued. "Ever heard 'em?" When Scanlon shook his head, Davy gave him a look that smacked of disappointment. "They're an old bluegrass family. The young ones are still playing the old stuff. You'd like it."

Scanlon knew better than to assume he was being invited to the barbecue. He was still too new in town. He waited for Davy to let the punch line drop.

"Addie's lookin' for someone to watch the feed store for her while everybody's at the barbecue. Said she'll pay six bucks an hour for three hours. Under the table. Won't be much to it—most everybody else in town will be at the barbecue."

Everybody but the new guy, Scanlon thought, tamping down a flash of annoyance. He'd known going into this undercover operation that it would be a long-term assignment. He couldn't expect an insular drug-dealing clan to take him to their bosom after a few months.

"I can do that," he said aloud.

"Good. I'll tell Addie you'll be there. Two o'clock on Saturday." Davy walked to the door and opened it. "She mentioned you by name, you know. Asked me to check with you specifically."

Scanlon smiled. "Tell her I said thanks. I sure can use the extra money."

Davy's gaze dropped to Scanlon's scarred hand. "Reckon the government's not exactly real generous these days."

"No. You'd think they'd want to do a little more to reward a fellow who took a bullet in their godforsaken wars."

"Just be at the feed store Saturday. Maybe if you do a good job then, Addie or one of the other Swains will find more jobs for you to do." Davy headed out the door, pulling it closed behind him.

Scanlon released a long, slow breath. Not quite what he'd expected when he'd spotted Davy McCoy coming out of the woods.

But was his sense of relief premature? The Swains had been plying their criminal trade for a lot of years now. They might not be brain surgeons, but they were as wily and vicious as the coyotes Davy McCoy liked to hunt.

Maybe they really didn't suspect his involvement in helping Isabel get away. But he couldn't afford to assume he was safe from scrutiny. He had to figure out a way to get Isabel back to safety as soon as possible.

For his sake as well as hers.

Chapter Three

The closet seemed to grow darker as time passed, despite the thin shaft of light drifting into the cramped space from the bedroom outside. The odor of old cedar tickled her nose, threatening more than once to make her sneeze. She had held the urge in check, hearing heavy footfalls from the hall that she knew didn't belong to Ben Scanlon.

The ache in her head had eased a little, probably thanks to the food he'd insisted she put in her stomach to dilute the effects of whatever drug her ambushers had injected into her. Her memory was starting to leach back into her brain as well; at least the moments preceding whatever had happened to her.

She'd gone out of her room at some point that morning. She remembered getting ice and then— something. Something had happened after she went to get the ice.

But what?

She pressed the heels of her hands against her forehead. She'd carried the ice bucket out of the room, down the hall—her room wasn't far from the elevators, but the ice maker was all the way down the hall, near the stairs—

An image flashed into her mind. A reflection of herself in the mirrored back of an elevator car. She looked tired and bedraggled in the image, dressed in sloppy clothes, with no makeup and her hair in a messy ponytail.

That meant something. Why did it mean something?

Had she gone somewhere on the elevator?

No, not on the elevator. She'd gone to the elevator alcove to get out of sight. Hadn't she?

But why had she wanted to be out of sight?

Swallowing a growl of frustration, she retraced her steps. Out the hotel room door. Down the hall, ice bucket in hand.

She'd dropped her key card. She could hear it hit softly on the vinyl flooring in front of the ice machine. She'd bent to pick it up—

And looked behind her on purpose. At the man.

Sandy hair. Black T-shirt. Faded jeans. Just like the man she'd spotted in the woods behind Scanlon's house.

"Isabel?"

Scanlon's quiet voice made her jump. Heart jackrabbiting, she answered in an equally soft voice, "Yeah?"

"It's safe to come out now."

She grabbed the doorknob and hauled herself

unsteadily to her feet to let herself out. The dim bedroom seemed unbearably bright, forcing her to squint.

She spotted Scanlon a few feet from the door, studying her with troubled blue eyes. He looked as if he was about to speak again, but she preempted him. "I know where I saw that man outside your house before."

"I do, too," Scanlon said bluntly. "I'm pretty sure he's one of the men who ambushed you this morning at the hotel." He reached out and brushed a clump of curls out of her eyes. "Cooper, as soon as I can get in touch with Brand, we're getting you out of here and back home to your family."

The idea of returning home to the pretty little farmhouse in Gossamer Ridge, Alabama, that she'd bought a couple of months earlier was only partially tempting. She had finally begun to think of Chickasaw County as home again, after so many years away. And she'd loved the stately old house on sight.

But being back with Scanlon again, feeling the crackle of danger filling the air around them with every passing second, she realized how much she'd lost when that warehouse in Virginia had blown up and ripped him out of her life.

Being with him here, both alive, both in trouble, was like taking her first full, sweet breath after drowning in grief for so many long, excruciating months.

No matter what lies he'd told her, what secrets he

was keeping now, she knew she couldn't walk away from him and return to the new life she'd built in Chickasaw County. She was his partner. Lies or no lies, watching his back was her job.

"No," she said, her voice strong and firm. "Whatever you've gotten into here, you need backup. You need me."

"Cooper—"

"Shut up, Scanlon. I'm not going anywhere."

"I'M NOT SURE IT'S A BAD idea," Adam Brand told Scanlon an hour of futile argument later.

"Not a bad idea?" Scanlon gripped the satellite phone more tightly, pressing his lips into a thin line at the sight of Isabel's look of triumph. He turned his back to her and lowered his voice. "Have you lost your mind?"

"You were a good team once. Who says you can't be again?" Brand's voice sounded tinny and faint over the satellite. Non-emergency communications between Scanlon and his SAC were supposed to be rare and carefully scheduled, carried out only over the satellite phone, which Scanlon kept locked in a metal box hidden beneath a loose floorboard in the linen closet.

"If the Swains discover she's here—"

"Don't let that happen," Brand said reasonably. "They don't make a lot of visits there—"

"They visited today." Scanlon told Brand about Davy McCoy's unexpected appearance.

"Sounds like a breakthrough to me," Brand said. "And the invitation came from Addie Tolliver herself?"

"That's what Davy said. I think it's a test."

"I'd concur."

"But I can't have Isabel staying here," Scanlon added, the extra layer of desperation in his voice having little to do with his worry about her safety.

He was still feeling the effects of the kiss he'd planted on his partner at the Fort Payne Mountain View Inn.

Right now, she was watching him with that excited grin she got when a case started going her way, and it was all he could do to keep from hanging up on Brand and hauling her back to his bedroom to kiss that smile off her smug little face. Six months away from her had done nothing to quench the passion he'd been nurturing for almost as long as he'd known her.

But Brand didn't know anything about those feelings. Isabel certainly didn't have a clue. He'd worked hard to keep his attraction to her carefully hidden, staying within the bounds of their professional relationship.

"You've been puzzling over those files for months now without being able to figure out if any of the Swains are even involved in last year's bombings. The bombings were Cooper's baby in the first place—let her do the profiling work while you're out in the field. She can give it a fresh eye."

Any other agent, and Scanlon would have agreed without another argument. He hated pushing around paper, looking for clues, much preferring to be out in the field.

But Cooper wasn't any other agent. "If they catch her here, we're both dead."

"So don't let them catch her," Brand responded, reprising his earlier argument.

Scanlon growled with frustration. "If I didn't know better, I'd think you planned this."

"Good thing you know better," Brand said.

"She's going to need clothes. A weapon."

"Maybe they left my Beretta and my clothes in my hotel room," Isabel suggested. "Can they look?"

Scanlon passed along the information to Brand.

"We've already secured her clothing. The Beretta was there, as well. But there's going to be the matter of her family. They'll be looking for her."

"That's why we should send her home to them. Let the bad guys think she got to a safe place and contacted her family."

"My brothers and sisters aren't going to believe just any old story," Isabel warned from her position near the stove. "You'll have to let me talk to one of them."

"Let her call one of them," Brand said.

"We can't take that chance—"

"I'll have the Huntsville office deliver a new phone with her clothes and her weapon when an agent comes to pick up the van this evening," Brand said calmly. "Let her call one of her family on the phone you've got." He hung up without warning.

Scanlon swore under his breath.

"Boy, didn't take long for you to go all lone wolf," Isabel said, her tone flippant. But he knew her well enough to recognize the hurt in her dark eyes.

"Everything here's so dangerous," he said quietly. "I don't want you in the middle of it."

"I'm trained to be in the middle of it." She lifted her chin, trying to look tough, but she wobbled a little, lingering weakness from the drug injection betraying her.

He couldn't hold back a smile, slipping his hand under her elbow to steady her. His fingers seemed to burn where he touched her. "I know."

"This investigation has to do with the serial bomber, doesn't it?" she asked, letting him lead her to the futon sofa.

He dropped beside her, allowing himself the secret pleasure of sitting close enough that their arms brushed when they moved. "It does," he admitted. "At least, we think it's connected. Either way, I'll be happy to bring the bastards down."

He had his own personal reasons for wanting the Swains to pay for their crimes, reasons that had nothing to do with the serial bomber investigation. Even Adam Brand didn't know what motivated him, as far as Scanlon knew. Then again, the wily SAC had a way of learning things only God himself could know.

"Well, you have plenty of time now to bring me up to speed." She nudged him with her shoulder, a light, friendly touch that shouldn't have sent fire pouring into his gut.

But it had. And now the memory of the kiss outside the hotel—the kiss she didn't even remember because she was so drugged up she could barely stand—assaulted his mind with a barrage of images designed to make him crazy.

He wanted to kiss her again, this time when she was conscious and would know what it meant when her lips pressed back against his. Her reaction to his kiss had caught him by surprise, a fierce, passionate response that had almost knocked him from his own feet.

Had she known it was him? Or had she been hallucinating some phantom lover, one she saw as more than just a partner and friend? The question had damned near begun to haunt him.

He crossed to the stove, needing distance from her. "At the time of the Virginia bombing, we'd already begun looking at older blasts that might fit the bomber's MO."

"Right—the explosion in Rome, Georgia, that killed a judge, and there was a bombing here in north Alabama—" She paused, her brow crinkling. "Are we still in north Alabama?"

"Yeah. A place called Bolen Bluff, about fifteen miles northeast of Fort Payne."

Her eyebrows notched upwards. "Jasper Swain's hometown."

Scanlon nodded. "Exactly."

"But Swain's been in jail for over twenty years," she said. "We talked about the possibility of a copy-cat, but—"

"But the Swains are concentrating on meth and weed these days," he finished for her. "I know. But the MO was so close to the Swain bombings. And the bomb in Virginia happened only after we started snooping into the Swains' business."

"You think they targeted us specifically?"

"Targeted *you*," he said flatly. He'd let her run the investigation into Jasper Swain's bombings, despite his own personal interest in the case. He'd even let her be the one to go visit Jasper at the jail in St. Clair County, afraid the old man might recognize him even after all these years.

Funny to think about now, considering he was living in the middle of the bloody Swains, trying to worm his way into the family business.

That had been Brand's idea, too. He'd seen a golden opportunity to kill off Scanlon's old self and create a whole new person for the undercover assignment he'd been thinking about for months.

"They're up to more than just drugs and protection down there," Brand had insisted soon after the bombing, while Scanlon had been hidden away at the SAC's hunting retreat in central Virginia. Scanlon had agreed to the undercover assignment and headed south to Alabama as soon as he recovered from the worst of his injuries.

Fortunately, he apparently looked different enough from the child he'd been the last time he was in Bolen Bluff that nobody had recognized him at all, at least as far as he knew.

"This was Brand's idea—sending you here." Isabel echoed his own thoughts so closely he had to smile. After years of working together, they'd formed the habit of finishing each other's sentences, their minds honed to think in similar directions.

It was the differences between them—her logical, scholarly approach contrasting with his more freewheeling, improvisational style—that had made them a good team. Brand had never tried assigning them to work with other agents after the first few times they'd worked together on cases.

"Yeah, Brand thinks the Swains may be up to more than just cooking meth and harvesting weed."

"Does he think the bombs in Georgia, Mississippi and Alabama are connected to the Swains, too?" she asked. "Did you finally make a connection between the victims?"

The bombing cases he and Isabel had been investigating centered on attacks on targets that, as far as they could tell, seemed completely random. The first had been the murder of a Georgia family court judge, which had seemed significant at the time in terms of motive—until the second bombing took

out the office of a small movie theater a few miles
west of Meridian, Mississippi.

A third blast had destroyed half a warehouse in
Gadsden, Alabama, and a fourth blew up a junkyard in western Birmingham. Only the judge died
in the bombings. The others had suffered property
damage only.

"We still haven't figured out any connection," he
admitted. "None of the people have any overt relationship to each other, and if there's a covert one,
we haven't come across it yet."

"I've thought about the cases from time to time,"
Isabel admitted, flashing him a faint smile. "You
know how I like a puzzle. But Jesse's kept me pretty
busy since I started working for him, and then there
was the business last month with my brother Rick
and his wife—"

"Rick got married?" The last Scanlon had heard,
Isabel's brother was having trouble settling in at
his new job with Cooper Security. Something about
personality conflicts with his brother, Jesse, who ran
the company.

"He did," she said, her smile widening. "He reconnected with someone he knew when he was
working at MacLear."

Isabel's brother Rick had worked for years at a
private security contractor, MacLear Enterprises,
before the company had been busted for running a
secret criminal enterprise under the table. The company owner, Jackson Melville, was under indictment

for the actions of the company's secret SSU—Special Services Unit—which had kidnapped a child and terrorized a woman from California.

Isabel's brother Rick had nothing to do with the SSU—according to Isabel, Rick hadn't even known the unit existed. But the entire company had collapsed under the weight of the allegations against Melville and the SSU, Rick's field operative position included.

"Was she another MacLear agent?" Scanlon asked.

"No—she was a CIA agent." She smiled at his arched eyebrow. "Apparently they got hot and heavy when they were both working out of Kaziristan about three years ago. They reconnected last month—she was targeted by assassins—"

"Boy, you die for a few months and you miss out on everything," he muttered drily.

"Oh! Did Brand tell you what we learned about the old MacLear SSU?"

Scanlon and his boss had conversed about little besides the undercover case he was working, and isolated as he was up here in the north Alabama mountains, Scanlon didn't have much access to news, either. He'd left his BlackBerry and laptop behind when he became Mark Shipley, the disabled vet with just enough disability pay to buy this ramshackle cabin in the middle of nowhere. "What about the SSU?"

"They're still operating. At least, the ones who

escaped indictment or capture. And they may be picking up new members."

Alarm rippled through him. "How do you know?"

"They went after Amanda—Rick's wife. Turns out Khalid Mazir, one of the candidates for president of Kaziristan, was an al Adar mole. Rick's wife, Amanda, was the only person outside al Adar who knew about Mazir's terrorist ties—the guy kidnapped and tortured her a few years ago. She got away, and I guess it wouldn't have mattered much if she hadn't seen Mazir's face."

"So she could identify him as an al Adar operative, which would mess with his plans to become president?"

"Exactly."

"And this guy hired SSU people to, what? Assassinate her?"

"Damned near succeeded," Isabel said with a grimace.

"I wonder if they were operating as far back as last summer," Scanlon mused.

"When the first bombing happened?"

He shrugged. "Probably not connected, but I know some of the SSU were explosives and munitions experts. What if they studied Jasper Swain's MO and decided to mimic it?"

Her brow creased in thought. "It's a pretty old fashioned MO. His style is primitive compared to the electronically triggered explosives available these days. Honestly, I don't know why anyone would use that kind of bomb if they had other options."

"Unless it's sentimental somehow."

"Sentimental?"

"Maybe the serial bomber is a fan of old Jasper. Maybe he builds the bombs the Swain way as a tribute."

Isabel looked skeptical. "Wouldn't a more famous bomber be a better choice? Someone like the Unabomber or Rudolph—"

Scanlon shook his head. "I don't know. I'm just spitballing at this point." He held out his hand to her, bracing himself for the feel of her warm, strong hand in his.

She took his hand, and the tingling commenced, but he managed not to let her see how she affected him as he pulled her to her feet. She gave him a quizzical look but followed as he led her into the hall.

"I keep the files in here." He opened the linen closet door and pulled up a loose floorboard. Besides the lockbox with the satellite phone, he also kept hidden a rectangular plastic box marked MISALGA, the Bureau shorthand for the bombing cases in Mississippi, Alabama and Georgia. He opened the box and handed her the thick portfolio where he kept copies of all the files on the case. "You up to a little light reading?"

She took the portfolio and grinned at him. "You bet."

They both turned to head back into the living room when a sound from the front of the house brought them up short.

A second later, someone knocked on the door.

"Closet," he said tersely, nodding toward the bedroom.

Holding onto the portfolio, Isabel disappeared behind the bedroom door, while Scanlon hurried to the living room and took a quick look at the porch through the window beside the door.

A curvy blond woman dressed in a linen suit stood in front of the door, glancing at her watch. Scanlon closed his eyes and released a sigh of frustration.

Dahlia was back.

"Mark, are you in there?"

He opened the door and pasted a smile on his face. "When did you get back in town?"

"Just a little while ago." Dahlia McCoy lifted to her tiptoes and brushed her pink lips against his. "I ran into Davy in town and he said you were home, so I thought I'd drop by to say hello before I go back to the office."

She entered without being asked, shrugging off her jacket to bare her toned, sun-kissed arms. She went straight to the refrigerator and pulled out a can of Diet Coke. Settling on the sofa as if she intended to stay awhile, she smiled at Scanlon.

He smiled back, hiding his dismay with the skill of a now-practiced liar.

He'd forgotten to tell Isabel about his girlfriend.

Chapter Four

That was definitely a woman's voice.

Isabel strained to hear what was going on in the front room. A purely academic interest, she reminded herself. Having Scanlon back as a partner temporarily didn't mean she had any right to question what he did with his personal life. If the woman even had anything to do with his personal life.

She made out Scanlon's low-pitched voice, followed by a woman's soft drawl. Isabel felt their footsteps shake the floor beneath her crossed legs as they entered Scanlon's bedroom.

"Wish I didn't have to go back to the office." The woman's sultry tone made Isabel's skin crawl. *Definitely girlfriend.*

Part of his undercover mission or window dressing? She doubted Scanlon had started a real relationship on assignment—not with the pressure of hiding his identity.

"It was sweet of you to come by and see me," Scanlon replied, his voice moving toward the door, as if he were trying to get her back out into the hall.

"I have a few more minutes," the woman said with a light laugh, followed by a silence that dragged on long enough for Isabel's mind to supply any number of stomach-turning scenarios for what was keeping Scanlon from saying something in return.

"Was your trip to Nashville a success?" he asked finally.

"Mmm."

Was that a yes or a no? Isabel wondered.

"Is that a yes or a no?" Scanlon asked.

"Why do you always want to talk about my job?" the woman asked, a hint of petulance in her voice.

Isabel rolled her eyes in the dark closet.

"It's a good job, sugar. You always dress so nice." Scanlon was really laying on the Texas drawl. "You must be doing important things."

You always dress so nice? Isabel grimaced. No wonder Scanlon couldn't keep a girlfriend. What self-respecting woman would find that an appealing compliment?

"You're so sweet," the woman said, answering Isabel's question. "But it would bore you to tears. All that tax and investment stuff. You don't care about that."

Scanlon had a master's degree in accounting, but he was letting this woman talk to him like he was nothing but a side of tasty beef. She *had* to be part of his undercover work.

Not that knowing his motives made it any easier to listen to her slobber all over him outside the closet door.

"Okay, big guy, time to get back to the office. You want to meet tonight at my place?"

"Not a good idea," Scanlon murmured. "I'm not sure Davy or any of the others would be happy to see us together."

"You're not Romeo, and Davy sure as hell isn't Tybalt."

"Who's Tybalt?" Scanlon asked.

Isabel strangled a laugh before it escaped her throat and exposed them both. Scanlon was the kind of hypereducated dork who quoted Spenser and Donne for fun. For Isabel, it was half his charm. Scanlon was playing the hell out of this poor woman. Isabel started to feel sorry for her, whoever she was.

"Just someone Romeo killed. I trust you won't be doing that to my brother?"

So, she was Davy's sister? Isabel strained to hear as they moved away from the bedroom. But the last thing she was able to make out was Scanlon's assurance that he didn't intend to go all Montague on the Capulets, though not in those exact terms.

She waited in the dark for Scanlon to give her the all clear, her mind supplying a picture of the girl with the drawl. Probably blonde—Scanlon gravitated toward the fairer-haired of the species. Curvy—he liked curves. She'd even seen him eyeing her own curves with appreciation, making her feel a little better about not fitting into those skinny jeans she liked to try on at the store but never ended up buying.

Smart, clearly Scanlon's usual type. Though not smart enough to know she was being played like a bloody violin....

"All clear." Scanlon said from just outside the closet.

Isabel let herself out and found her former partner on the edge of his bed, his elbows on his knees. He shot her a look of apology. "Guess I forgot to tell you about Dahlia."

Dahlia? Just perfect. "You forgot?"

"She's Davy McCoy's sister."

"I figured out that much myself," she said. *Are you sleeping with her?*

"I'm not sleeping with her," Scanlon said.

"Yet," she murmured.

"It's complicated."

"Since everyone thinks you're an injured vet, tell her the enemy messed up your plumbing, too," Isabel suggested.

Scanlon's lips curved. "Hadn't thought of that."

"Glad to help." She started out of the room.

"Cooper—" He caught her arm and pulled her to face him. His eyes were a smoky blue, liquid and inviting, like a mountain pool just begging for her to dive in and enjoy a long swim.

She hated what he could do to her with one devastating look. If her parents' wreck of a marriage had taught her anything, it was that giving someone that kind of power over you was a bad idea.

"I'm sorry," he said. "I should have given you warning."

"You have a right to a personal life."

"It's not personal with Dahlia."

She tried to ignore how much relief she felt from that one simple declaration. "Maybe not for you—"

His lips flattened. "Brand said she could be an asset."

Brand again, Isabel thought. Scanlon put a lot of stock in the SAC's opinion. Of course, she had, too, until about an hour ago when she'd learned about his heartless lies. "Is she part of the meth operation?"

"Not that I can tell. She works at an accounting firm in Fort Payne but lives here in Bolen Bluff. Her father is a retired coal miner with respiratory issues, and God knows she can't depend on Davy to look after the old man." There was a hint of affection in Scanlon's voice.

Maybe he liked Dahlia McCoy more than he realized?

"Just be careful," Isabel said aloud. "You break her heart, she may not be the only one who gets hurt."

Scanlon grimaced. "Especially if we're right about the Swains being involved with these bombings." He let go of her arm and backed away. "Why don't you lie down and take a nap? You've had a rough day."

His bed did look pretty inviting, she had to admit. She felt unsteady on her feet, and the ache in her head was still making a bit of a racket.

"Have you heard from Brand about my things?"

"I'll check in a minute," he said in the same soothing drawl he'd used with Dahlia earlier. She should smack him for playing her, as well, but she had to admit the tone of voice made her want to purr a little, too.

She sat on the edge of his bed and found the mattress springy and soft, adding to the temptation to just lie down and let her trouble melt away into sleep.

Scanlon's lips curved again as he apparently read her thoughts. She hated that about him, too, how he always saw through her when she was trying to play it tough. "Come on, Cooper, don't try to go all John Wayne on me. You can sleep a little while. The world won't fall apart without you."

He was echoing words she'd said to him before. It had been her father's favorite saying when she was little and fighting sleep. She'd used it on her partner a few times when he was driving himself into exhaustion on this case or that.

But she'd been wrong, hadn't she? Her world had fallen apart completely without him.

She lay on the bed, atop the covers, and closed her eyes, listening for the sound of Scanlon leaving the room. But she didn't hear him budge. She opened her eyes and found him standing at the side of the bed, watching her.

"If I'd been even a few minutes later this morning—" His voice came out ragged. Hoarse.

She sat up and caught his hand in hers, all anger fleeing in the face of his pain. "If I'd reached the office before you did and picked up that note you took off my desk—"

He squeezed her hand. "Sleep well." Bending, he pressed his lips against her forehead, the kiss chaste and sweet.

But as he walked out of the bedroom, an image flashed through her aching head, fuzzy and surreal.

Scanlon, wrapping his arms around her, pressing her back against something solid and hard. The door of a green panel van. She'd seen a panel van as they'd walked out into the morning sunlight, hadn't she? Angled into one of the slots across the dark gray asphalt of the hotel parking lot.

His arms were strong, his hands firm as they lifted to her face, holding her still. She could barely focus her eyes but found a way to hold his gaze, to see a miracle when she'd never really believed in miracles before.

He was alive. He was holding her close.

It was as if God had given her mercy.

Then his head dipped, his mouth descended, and she was on fire. Quivering where he touched her, burning from the inside out as the kiss deepened and she fell into madness.

She jerked into a sitting position, staring at the wall across from the bed. A low-slung dresser sat against the cracked Sheetrock, a scarred mirror affixed above the battered wooden top. In the mirror, her pale reflection stared back at her, one hand lifted to her lips.

Had that been a fantasy, a drug-induced hallucination?

Or had it been real?

For the first time, it hit her just how much she'd come to depend on having someone in her family around when she was feeling vulnerable and alone. Right now, she'd give anything to call her sister Megan on the phone—

The phone. Brand had told Scanlon to let her call her family to keep them from worrying.

She went to the front room, expecting to find Scanlon there, but he was nowhere around. Nor was the phone. Taking care not to let the curtain move too much, she looked outside the front window. She saw nothing. No one.

Releasing a sigh of frustration, she looked around the front room, wondering if he'd left the phone out where she could find it. Probably not—it was likely his only relatively secure means of communication with the FBI. He wouldn't want anyone in the Swain clan to know he had it.

Thinking back, she remembered the loose floorboard in the hall closet. He'd hidden files underneath—was the phone there, too?

She checked under the board and discovered a rectangular lock box with something inside that rattled when she moved the box. The phone? The lock didn't budge when she tried to open the box, so she headed into the kitchen for something she could use to pick it open, walking into the room just as the front door opened.

The urge to flee propelled her backward into the hallway before her brain registered that the newcomer was just Scanlon, coming in with a couple of firewood logs under one arm.

She sagged against the hallway wall. "You need one of those bells around your neck so I'll know you're coming."

His gaze dipped to the box in her hands. "What are you doing with that?"

His tone made her blink. "Calling home. Isn't that what we agreed I should do, before my family gets wind of my disappearance and makes a stink?"

His expression relaxed a little. "I thought you were going to take a nap first."

She returned to the kitchen, handing him the box. "Thought I'd better get on this before it gets too much later. I usually call one of my brothers or sisters at least once a day. They'll start worrying if I don't check in."

He punched in a code on the box's digital lock, slanting a look at her, a faint smile on his face. The box clicked open, revealing the satellite phone, and he handed it to her. "What are you going to tell them?"

"To tell people I escaped and got to a safe place, called my family and one of them came and got me. No police involved."

"Why wouldn't you call the police?"

"Because I had drugs in my system when they found me, and my family didn't want me to get arrested."

He looked skeptical, so she added, "I was talking crazy about being kidnapped and shot up with drugs." Meeting his gaze directly, she added a pointed elaboration. "I've been acting odd lately anyway—see, my partner just got killed a few months ago by a bomb meant for me, and I've been eaten up with guilt and all, blaming myself for his horrible death—"

His stricken look pricked her conscience with remorse for getting in a dig at his expense.

"Okay, I get it. Can they sell that story?"

"It only has to be sold if someone asks any questions, right? One of them will go to the hotel and check me out. Hopefully Brand's already sent my stuff—"

"I talked to Brand a few minutes ago—the stuff should be here tonight around nine. They try to make their deliveries during night hours when they can."

"Where is the drop site?"

"An abandoned barn down the road. It's on my property, so I can't let stuff stay there for long. The van's already been sitting in that barn a lot longer than I'm comfortable with."

He looked older than the last time she'd seen him, she realized. She supposed living a constant lie under threat of death would do that to anyone.

And Scanlon was a man who let things eat at him, even in the best of times. He always seemed to be nursing secret troubles. It took a long time after their first case together for him to start letting her in on some of the secrets.

Of the two of them, she was by far the more stoic and rational, the one who found ways to distance herself from some of the horrors they saw in their line of work. She had to be able to do that, or she didn't think she could cope. Her inability to distance herself from Scanlon's death had led her to leave the Bureau.

But Scanlon always felt things. Everything. At times, she'd wondered how he survived it without going insane.

"You want some privacy?" he asked, nodding at the phone.

Afraid she'd fall apart the second she heard a familiar voice, she nodded. Scanlon smiled and carried the firewood into the hallway. She heard his footsteps recede as he entered the bedroom and closed the door behind him.

She took a deep breath and dialed her sister's

phone number at the office. Megan answered on the second ring. "Cooper Security, Megan Randall speaking."

"Hey, Meggie, it's Isabel."

"Izzy! Thank God—I've been trying to call your cell phone all day. Where have you been?"

"Is something wrong? Why've you been trying to reach me?"

"Luke called a little before lunch—the U.S. attorney has decided not to indict Barton Reid at the moment." Megan was talking about their cousin, Luke Cooper, who'd suffered a few harrowing days on the run from the MacLear SSU operatives Barton Reid had sent after him and his wife, Abby.

Isabel's gut tightened with outrage. "How can they not indict the guy? He sent a bunch of goons to kidnap a two-year-old to get his mother to cooperate with their cover-up!"

"The evidence just isn't there, or so the U.S. attorney says. Luke's furious, Sam's threatening to air all the dirty laundry of the U.S. attorney's office—"

Sam was Luke's brother and a former U.S. attorney himself. "Is there anything we can do?"

"Just prove the connection between Reid and the SSU, but everybody who could testify to that fact is either in hiding or dead." Megan's answer came out in a low growl. "Sorry to spring that on you. By the way, where are you calling from? I don't recognize the number."

Isabel settled on the futon sofa before her wobbling knees gave out. "Are you sitting down?"

Megan's voice grew wary. "Yeah."

"I'm in a cabin in the woods. I can't tell you exactly where. But I'm with Ben Scanlon."

There was utter silence on the other end of the line.

"I'm not crazy," Isabel added quickly. "Although I was hallucinating as recently as a few hours ago—"

"What?" Megan asked.

As succinctly as she could, Isabel summed up the last few hours, from the abduction she knew must have happened—but couldn't quite remember—to waking up on a futon sofa, staring across the kitchen at a man she'd thought she'd buried only six months earlier. "He's alive and he's fine. And I'm a little freaked out by it all, but I'm okay."

"Oh, sweetie, I don't know whether to laugh or cry!" Of all of Isabel's siblings, Megan was the only one who knew just how hard she'd been taking the loss of her partner. A widow herself, Megan was still dealing with the grief of her husband's death during what was supposed to be a low-threat peacekeeping tour of duty in Kaziristan.

"I'm okay now. The shock has worn off."

"You're going to stay there?" Megan sounded worried.

"I can help him." She told Megan the cover story she had come up with. "Nobody can know where I am except the family."

"But there are people who are willing to grab you out of a hotel in broad daylight and spirit you to God knows where—"

"Even more reason to stick around and find out what's going on, don't you think?" Isabel glanced up to find Scanlon in the doorway, looking at her. He tapped his watch. "I need to get off the phone now. I love you. Be sure everyone in the family knows the cover story so they'll know what to say if anyone comes around asking questions."

"I will. Love you, too, Izzy. Bye!"

Isabel held out the phone to Scanlon, blinking back the tears burning in her eyes. He took the phone, stuck it in the back pocket of his jeans and crouched in front of her, his thumb brushing across a tear that had slipped out of her steely control to trickle down her cheek.

"You don't have to stay here if you don't want to," he said quietly, his thumb sliding over the curve of her cheek, settling in front of her ear as he threaded his fingers through her curls. His other hand rose to cradle her face. "You've been through a hell of a lot in just a few hours, and there's no shame in taking yourself out of the game."

She shook her head, fighting her emotions. "I'm in this. I need to know who ambushed me. I don't know what they want, but they clearly wanted something. We should find out what it is. It might be exactly what you need to bring this investigation to a close and get your life back."

His eyes darkened as his gaze leveled with hers. "I just want you safe. It's what I've wanted from the beginning of this whole mess."

Her heart contracted. "Scanlon—"

His head dipped. For a second, she was certain he was going to kiss her. But he froze in place, his gaze falling to rest on her parted lips. "Damn it, Cooper—"

It was a familiar point in time, she realized. A point of no return, when the tension buzzing between them could take on a new and dangerous tenor. They'd reached this point before, during long and harrowing cases when the whole world seemed to be spinning out of control. Moments when a little human connection provided a temptation almost too exquisite to resist.

But one of them always moved. Always backed away before they did something that couldn't be undone. She waited for the inevitable retreat, for Scanlon to pull away and rise to his feet, putting distance and cold air between them.

That moment never came.

Scanlon lowered his head slowly, until his lips brushed against hers. Just a light touch. A question.

She stood on the precipice of change, terrified and exhilarated. One step forward and the world would drop from beneath her feet, plunging her into free-fall. It could be amazing—or disastrous.

But if there was one thing she'd learned from

the last six months, it was the price of regret. The haunting specter of things left unsaid.

She laid her hand on his chest, curling her fingers in the soft fabric of his flannel shirt. Slowly, deliberately, she slanted her mouth over his, brushing her tongue against his lower lip. He growled low in his throat and snaked one arm around her waist, pulling her flush to his body.

In a heartbeat, the world dropped away, and she fell.

Chapter Five

At some point, they shifted positions, though Scanlon couldn't remember when or how. He only knew that when his brain caught up with his body, he was seated on the futon with Isabel straddling his lap, her dark curls falling like a curtain around them. She drew back for a second, her tea-colored eyes drunk with desire, and ran her forefinger across his bottom lip.

"Are we crazy to be doing this?" she asked, breathless.

"Yes," he said, because anything else would be a lie. Of all the times they could have chosen to take this step, now had to be the worst option possible. He was undercover in the middle of a deadly clan of rural crank cookers, and Isabel was on their hit list for reasons neither of them could fathom.

Why were they taking this chance?

As if she could read the cold dose of reality beginning to overwhelm his thoughts, she cradled his face between her slender hands and kissed him again, with more tenderness than raw passion.

He gave in, disarmed by her bravery, by his own wretched loneliness for her.

He'd missed her desperately, the way she grounded him when he started to go too far off the mark in their investigations. He'd found himself talking to her so many times, in the dark solitude of his bedroom at night, looking to the still, small voice of her memory to keep him on the right track.

"I'm sorry," he whispered against her lips.

She drew back, arching her dark eyebrows.

"All this time alone here, I knew you were okay. And I still missed the hell out of you." He threaded his fingers through the dark tangle of curls that had always fascinated and tempted him. "If you missed me even half as much, and you thought I was dead and you'd never see me again—"

"I missed you more." Her voice vibrated with pain, and he pulled her to him, pressing his lips against her forehead.

"I'm sorry. Brand and I were wrong not to tell you."

She eased off his lap and onto the futon cushion beside him. "Yeah, you were. And what we just did—I thought it would change everything, but it doesn't really. Does it?"

"Because I lied about being dead?" He wasn't sure he was following her train of thought, which scared him a little, because by the end of their days as partners, they'd gotten pretty good at reading each other's minds.

"Because of the lie. Because you're someone named Mark Shipley now, and you have a girl-friend who sure as hell doesn't need to smell another woman on you at the wrong time—" She pushed her hair away from her face with a small growl of frustration. "And, frankly, because I don't think romantic relationships ever really work, no matter how I pretend they do. Something always happens to screw things up."

"Your mom screwed up, Cooper. She couldn't handle being a housewife with six kids and a husband who risked his life for a living. That doesn't mean you'll make the same mistakes." He gave her a nudge with his shoulder, making her smile.

"Based on the last twenty-four hours, I'm not exactly looking mistake-proof."

"You got away from the bad guys, even hopped up on something that was making you see pink elephants."

She grimaced. "Melting eyeballs, but close enough."

"Besides, sometimes relationships do work out. My mom's still married to my dad." He hesitated slightly over the last word. Technically, Bill Scanlon wasn't his father. But he'd adopted his new wife's son when Scanlon had been a young boy, gave him a new name and a good life.

"The exception that proves the rule."

"Now you're just being stubborn."

She slanted a skeptical look at him. "The guy who believes three dates and out is a viable rule of romantic relationships, arguing for happily ever after? Give me a break."

Fair enough, he supposed. He hadn't been one for long-term relationships, not because he didn't believe they were possible but because he knew they were. He knew that falling in love, trying to build a life with a woman was an all-or-nothing proposition. He couldn't give anything only half of himself. He wasn't wired that way.

And all he'd had room for since he was a young boy was his search for answers. Even his work at the FBI had been undertaken in service of his real goal, a goal neither Isabel nor Adam Brand knew anything about.

He was determined to find out who had murdered his father twenty-five years ago.

When Scanlon had been a boy of eight, his biological father, Sheriff Bennett Allen of Halloran County, Alabama, had been murdered outside their family home right here in Bolen Bluff. Scanlon had witnessed it, but he'd never been able to remember the actual moment of the shooting.

He'd heard a car engine but could remember seeing nothing after that until he looked down at his feet to see his father bleeding out on the driveway, three large holes in his chest.

"No answer for that?" Isabel asked in a deceptively light tone, though her eyes darkened with dread at his answer.

She might think she was cynical about romance,

but she wanted to believe it could happen. That forever could be real and attainable. Hopeless little romantic.

But as tempting as the thought might be, he couldn't be her prince. Not until he had his answers. And he sure as hell had no right to ask her to put her life on hold while he chased those dragons around the woods and valleys of Bolen Bluff.

"You're right," he said bluntly, hating the way she seemed to shrink from him, as if preparing herself for a body blow. "I'm not in any position to argue for true love. And you're right that this is really bad timing. I don't even know why I agreed with Brand that you should stick around here a couple of days. You should be home with your family, where it's safe."

"I can help you."

"That doesn't mean you should."

"It's my choice."

He wanted to kiss her again. Or throttle her. He wasn't sure which emotion had the upper hand at the moment. "We should rustle up something for dinner. You barely ate any soup."

"I'm still not that hungry."

"What is it you're always telling me—food is fuel?"

Her lips curved slightly at his recitation of one of her favorite bromides. "Dad always says that."

"Your dad's a wise man." He clapped his hand lightly on her knee and pushed to his feet. "You want another go at the soup or would you like to try something a little heartier?"

"I'll have whatever you were planning to eat for dinner," she said, angling her chin upward as if she had just agreed to take on the lions in the Roman Coliseum.

"I went fishing last weekend and lucked into a school of hungry crappie." He pulled the wrapped fillets from the freezer and started running hot water over them.

She crossed to the refrigerator and tugged it open, frowning as she took in the mostly bare interior. "Where do you keep your vegetables?"

"In cans, where the good Lord intended." He waved at the cabinet next to the sink.

She rolled her eyes at him, as he'd known she would. At the familiar reaction, a feeling of well-being flooded his system, threatening to overwhelm all good sense.

This was right, no matter the arguments against her staying. This was where she belonged. At his side, his partner, always.

But deep down, he knew the whole situation was anything but right, and the last—the worst—place Isabel Cooper should be was anywhere near him or Halloran County.

AFTER A DINNER OF FISH and canned turnip greens, Scanlon spent the next couple of hours trying to talk Isabel into an early bedtime while she ignored him and started scanning the files he'd kept hidden under the closet floorboard.

She didn't know how long it would be smart or safe for either of them to remain in Halloran County, and if she could speed up the process of getting Scanlon out of here and back to the safety of the D.C. field office, she was going to do it, even if it meant yawning through a few dry reports about the southern Appalachian drug trade.

She already knew that Halloran County, along with the other counties encompassing the Alabama Piedmont area, had a drug problem. Most places with pockets of poverty and clannish insularity did. She also knew the Swain family appeared to be a notch above the usual toothless, brainless idiot who cooked his crank in the kitchen of his own house with a dirty-diapered baby or three playing on the floor at his feet. The Swains had organized into an actual crime family, formed their own little redneck Mafia in the hills of Halloran County.

What she wasn't sure about, however, was whether or not their bomb-throwing days had ended when the patriarch, Jasper Swain, had been sent up for life a quarter century ago.

"All the research suggests the bombings stopped cold when old Jasper went to prison," she said a little later, when Scanlon came into the kitchen where she sat at the small card table, going over the files. "If the serial bomber is connected to the

Swains, he didn't start striking until a couple of years ago."

Scanlon stopped by the table and bent over her shoulder, looking over her notes. He smelled good. It was the same familiar, masculine scent she'd always noticed when he was around, one she'd attributed to whatever aftershave he used before arriving at work crisp, clean-shaven and ready to work. But the beard stubble that brushed against her temple as he pulled back ruled out the idea that he'd shaved.

She guessed it was just how he always smelled.

Even if he hadn't shaved, he'd changed clothes, she noticed as she turned to look at him. He had donned a pair of black trousers and a long-sleeved black T-shirt tight enough to emphasize how lean and muscular he'd become over the past six months. He'd never been a slouch in the physical department, but he was damned near ripped now, and she didn't think he was sneaking trips to the gym out here.

"How do people around here think you support yourself?" she asked, curiosity overcoming her desire to focus on the case.

"I do some carpentry work here and there, under the table. Supposedly I'm on disability because of my 'war injury.'" He made a face as he said it. "War injury. As if it compares to what real soldiers go through."

"I think real soldiers figure we're all on the same side in the same war. We all protect this country the best we can."

His hand moved toward her, as if he wanted to brush his knuckles against her cheek. She braced herself for the touch, but it never came. He dropped his hand back to his side and cleared his throat. "I'm heading down to the drop point to pick up the new sat phone and leave the other one there for the agents to pick up on their next trip out. Your stuff should be there by now, too."

She wished she could go with him. She didn't like the idea of him out there with nobody watching his back. But he'd been handling this case on his own for six months, and so far he was still standing. And if the people who'd tried to grab her from the hotel in Fort Payne spotted her out in the woods with Scanlon, they'd both be dead before they could run for cover.

"Be careful," she said as he opened the door.

He turned and looked at her. "You hear anything—anything at all—you know where to hide. I have a Glock hidden in the top drawer of the bedside table. Use it if you need it."

He closed the door behind him, leaving her alone in the silence of the empty cabin. She sat for a minute, feeling the quiet sink down around her like a blanket of heavy fog, cold and oppressive. She forced her attention back to the files, but not before she lifted a quick, silent prayer for Scanlon's safety.

SPRING WAS IN FULL BLOOM in north Alabama, but the nights remained chilly and, on this particular evening, damp as well. Clouds scudding across the night sky blocked the moonlight, making for a treacherous hike down the mountain to the battered old pine barn where he'd left the borrowed van earlier that day.

The van was gone, he saw with relief, feeling a weight slough off his shoulders. In its place, tucked nonchalantly against the side of the rickety structure, was a large olive-drab knapsack that had seen better days.

He took a quick look inside the main compartment and the pockets. The outer pockets contained the new satellite phone and a compact Beretta—Isabel's weapon. So Rawlings and whichever Swain clan thugs went with him had left Isabel's weapon behind at the hotel. He didn't know whether to consider that choice odd or not.

He picked up the knapsack and laid the old satellite phone where it had sat, hiding the device beneath some rotted hay and windblown leaves. Looking deeper inside the knapsack's main compartment, he found that the Huntsville resident agents had rolled Isabel's clothes into compact coils, the better to fit them into the knapsack. On top of the clothes sat a folded sheet of paper with Isabel's name written on the outside.

He debated whether or not to read the note for about two seconds before he took the risk of flicking on the small penlight attached to his key ring.

He unfolded the note and ran the light over the contents, reading quickly.

It was from Rick—one of Isabel's brothers. The one who'd just gotten married to the former CIA agent, he recalled. The note was terse but informative—Rick had known a MacLear operative named J. T. Swain when they'd both worked for the security company. Swain had left MacLear shortly before the company was caught up in the SSU scandal, but rumor had it Swain was one of the SSU operatives. He'd had a reputation of being dangerous and reckless—which certainly fit the Swains whom Scanlon had met in the past six months.

It was possible, even likely, that J. T. Swain had nothing to do with Halloran County's Swains at all. But it was definitely worth looking into.

He shoved the note back into the knapsack and zipped the bag up. Checking carefully before leaving the dilapidated barn, he headed out into the night, the knapsack over his shoulder.

Still mulling the possibility that the Swains might have connections to the MacLear Special Services Unit, Scanlon almost stumbled into Davy McCoy and Bobby Rawlings trudging through the woods ahead of him. His heart jumping into his throat, he hunkered down behind a clump of wild hydrangea and waited in silence for them to pass.

Their voices carried a little in the cool night air, although Scanlon caught only snippets of their conversation until they were just a few yards away.

From what he could make out, Davy was blasting Bobby for letting Isabel get away.

As they got closer, Bobby lashed back in words so profane it made even Scanlon's eyebrows raise, accusing Davy and someone else, someone he called "Jay," of not being able to take an elbow to the groin, though in far more colorful terms. Davy snapped back that Bobby ran like a turtle and let a drugged-out girl outpace him.

Knowing Bobby and his deadly anger, Scanlon expected the man's answer to be a right hook, but Bobby just spat out the most interesting—and terrifying—thing Scanlon had heard in hours. "Don't matter why she got away. We better find her, and fast. If we don't find out where she's keepin' it, we're as good as dead."

Keeping what? Scanlon listened even more attentively.

"Jay should have given her a bigger dose of Special K," Davy argued.

Special K, Scanlon thought. Ketamine. Now he knew what they'd injected into her.

"Carmela at the hotel said somebody picked up her stuff to take home to her. So why don't we just head on down to Gossamer Ridge and take care of her there? That's probably where she's hidin' the damned thing anyway." Davy sounded peeved. He had a chip on his shoulder anyway, his lack of blood ties putting him firmly on the outer edges of the

Swain clan. Having Bobby lord it over him only made him feel more aggrieved.

So, they were looking for something they thought Isabel had. But what? Did she know about it? Was that one of the things she'd forgotten about the attack?

"God, would you quit with the whinin'?" Bobby growled. A thwacking sound followed—had he hit Davy?

Apparently so, for suddenly the underbrush ahead of Scanlon's hiding place erupted with furious scuffling. Scanlon froze in place, terrified their fisticuffs would inadvertently reveal his hiding place.

Suddenly, a shotgun boomed, the noise splitting the night air. Scanlon ducked on instinct, his heart slamming against his sternum, but at least the scuffling came to a halt.

A low female voice followed in the wake of the shotgun reverberation. "What the hell do you boys think you're doing?"

Elusive memory niggled at the back of Scanlon's mind. The woman's voice seemed familiar, but he couldn't place it. It was an older voice, deep and authoritative. Her distinctive hill-country accent pegged her as a local, probably from a long line of people who'd inhabited this area since the days of the early settlers. She almost certainly had to be a Swain, or someone connected to them, and yet he couldn't quite place the voice.

He wished he dared to peek around the edge of

the bush that gave him camouflage, but that was a sure way to end up dead.

"Get your sorry hides back home 'fore I set the others on you, you hear? You got things you left undone, and rollin' around in the dirt like a couple of snot-nosed babies ain't gettin' it done."

Scanlon heard Davy and Bobby scramble to their feet and head off in the woods. But had the woman moved? He heard a soft rustle, as if someone was still out there, just a few feet away, walking through the underbrush.

He found he was holding his breath and let it go silently.

Finally the soft swishing noises moved slowly away, and he dared a quick look from behind the sheltering bush.

Davy and Bobby were already out of sight, but the woman, whoever she was, remained in sight, about twenty yards away. She had her back to him, but he could make out a thickset figure, dressed in dark colors, moving up the hill toward the main Swain conclave that lay on the other side of the crest.

He waited until she was out of sight before he moved, edging through the woods like a soldier on a reconnaissance mission, using trees, bushes and rock outcroppings as cover until he reached the edge of the clearing around his house.

All the way, his mind worried with the new piece of information he'd gleaned from the conversation he'd overheard. He'd assumed their attack on Isabel was motivated by revenge for her work trying to tie them to the serial bombings. But he should have known that was far too weak a motive to draw the Swains from their Halloran County comfort zone.

They believed Isabel had something they wanted. Believed it enough to risk kidnapping her from her very public hotel and carrying her off to—what? Torture her until she gave them the information they wanted? So whatever it was they thought she had, it was significant. Something they considered a threat.

Something they'd kill for.

Chapter Six

"J. T. Swain." Isabel frowned. "What's the likelihood a Swain would bother leaving here to work for a living when they can stay, cook all the crank and grow all the weed they want, and bully people around for the rest of their lives?"

"Worth looking into." Scanlon looked troubled, and she didn't think Rick's note was the source of his concern.

"Is there something else?" she asked.

He pulled up a folding chair and sat. "I almost ran into Davy McCoy and Bobby Rawlings in the woods."

"They didn't see you, did they?"

"No. I hid before they could. But they came pretty close." His frown deepened. "They were talking about screwing up what happened this morning at the hotel."

This morning? It seemed as if she'd been here with Scanlon for days, not hours. "Did you find out what happened?"

"You still don't remember anything?"

"Only images, like from dreams." Elusive ones, making her edgy with frustration. "What did you hear?"

"Davy and someone named Jay were on either side of you while you were drugged, trying to take you out by the stairs. Bobby was behind, watching their backs and flanks. You must have dropped and elbowed them in the groins to get away, and Bobby didn't move fast enough to catch up with you."

Another image flashed in her mind—a twisty tunnel. "I ran down a hallway. It was like being underground—so strange—"

"That was the ketamine talking."

"They gave me ketamine?" She shuddered. "No wonder I was hallucinating. I'm lucky they didn't overdose me."

"Davy thinks they didn't dose you enough. Apparently you were a handful, even drugged out of your skull." He flashed her a smile, but his expression faded to worry quickly.

"What else aren't you telling me?" she prodded.

"Why they ambushed you in the first place."

She arched an eyebrow. "Why?"

He looked reluctant to tell her. "According to Davy and Bobby, you have something they want."

She frowned. "Like what?"

"They never said. But Davy suggested heading to Gossamer Ridge to get it, which means it must be something pretty damned big to risk a move like that."

No wonder he looked worried. "That's crazy."

"You don't have any idea what it could be?"

"Not a clue." Her eyes felt gritty, and her head ached. Ketamine had a pretty long recovery period, if she remembered her drug facts. No wonder she'd felt awful all day.

Scanlon seemed to read her thoughts. "Take a shower and change into something clean." He picked up the knapsack he'd brought with him from the drop site. "I'm afraid whatever needs washing will have to be cleaned by hand. Can't risk taking a load of women's clothes to the coin laundry in town. You can dry what you wash in front of the hearth in the bedroom."

A shower and clean clothes sounded like a wonderful idea. She took the knapsack from him, her fingers brushing his in the exchange. She darted a quick look at him and found herself the object of his intense gaze.

Her stomach coiling into a fiery knot, she glanced at the futon. "If you'll get the futon folded out, I'm going to try to get some sleep when I'm finished showering."

"Take my bed. I'll sleep out here."

She shot a skeptical look at the futon. It was barely big enough for her, much less a man who had five inches and seventy pounds on her. "I'll take the futon," she said firmly. "You're the one who has to go out and move around town. Don't want to have to explain why you're all hunched up like Quasimodo."

"But there's a door to the outside here. There's not one in the bedroom, which will give you time to get in the closet if someone breaks in."

"If someone breaks in, won't they wonder why you're sleeping on the futon and not the bed?"

"I could say I just fell asleep watching TV." He shot her a grim smile. "And then I could just ask them what they're doing breaking into my house in the first place."

He had a point. But the futon was going to be hell on his back. "We could share the bed."

His eyebrow darted up a notch.

"We shared a hotel room once, remember?"

"With two beds, not one."

And it had been hard not to crawl into bed with him even then, at a time long before she'd admitted to herself that she was starting to have not-so-partner-like feelings for Scanlon. Now that she'd gotten a taste of his passion, she knew sleeping in the same bed without consequences was damned near impossible.

"We could take turns," she suggested. "I sleep a few hours, then I spell you—"

"I've slept on the futon before. I lived. I'll live again. Just go take your shower and stop worrying about me."

She retreated to the bathroom and dug through the knapsack to see what the FBI had managed to pack for her while she waited for the water to run hot in the tub. There was a set of dirty clothes in a plastic bag. She set that aside. She also found the gold locket that had once belonged to her childhood friend, Annie. Curling the chain around her wrist, she reached back into the knapsack and pulled out clean underwear, a soft pair of sweats and a University of Alabama T-shirt.

That ought to cool the ardor of any would-be lover, she thought with a grimace, laying the locket atop the pile of clothes and getting into the shower.

The hot water beating down on her body felt like heaven. She scrubbed and shampooed quickly, a little worried her still-wobbly legs wouldn't hold her up for long. Rinsing off, she found her mind wandering to the files she'd been going over while she waited for Scanlon to return from the drop site.

The key was finding the connection between the bombings. The problem, however, was that there was no connection at all that anyone had been able to establish. The Georgia judge hadn't known the Mississippi movie theater owner, and neither had known the Alabama junkyard operator or the warehouse owner. None of the businesses were connected even tangentially. No common parent company or any common vendors or suppliers.

The only connection seemed to be the bomber himself.

She went still in the shower. What if the bomber *was* the only connection? What did that do to their profile?

A bomber would have to have a reason to kill a

judge or bomb a movie theater, even if he was just a sociopath who liked to wreak havoc. He'd have a reason that meant something to him. That was the premise on which they'd built their profile.

But what if the motivation was money?

That small detail would change everything.

Stepping out of the tub, she grabbed a couple of well-worn towels from the linen shelf, too excited by her new theory to stop and dress. She wrapped one towel around her wet hair and the larger around her body, shoved her clothes back into the knapsack and dashed out in search of Scanlon.

Hearing noise in the bedroom, she burst in, sliding to a stop at the sight of Scanlon standing by the bed, stripped to a pair of black boxers. He turned at the sound of her arrival, his eyes widening.

Looking down, she saw the towel barely covered her body and was peeking open to reveal most of her left leg.

"Is something wrong?" he asked, looking alarmed.

"No. Sorry." Her whole body grew warm, and not just from embarrassment. She'd seen Scanlon nearly naked before—they often swam together at the gym—but she almost felt as if she were ogling a stranger. He'd always looked good, with a lean swimmer's body. But his muscles were now rock hard and defined, as if he'd spent time working on getting them into shape.

She spotted a set of dumbbells tucked in the corner of the room that she hadn't noticed before in her quick trips to the hiding closet. He'd been working out, clearly.

Gearing up for a coming battle?

Her gaze tried to return to Scanlon's whipcord body, but she forced her eyes up to meet his gaze instead, and found him looking at her bare legs. She gathered the towel more tightly around her and cleared her throat. "I had a thought in the shower. About the connection between the bombings."

He snapped his gaze up to hers, a hint of sheepish color tinting his cheeks. "Yeah?"

"You know how the SSU went after my cousin and his wife?"

"Yeah—"

"Well, the SSU had nothing against Abby and Luke. They had no inherent beef against them. So why'd they go after them?"

"Because Barton Reid paid them to."

"Exactly," she said with a grin.

Understanding flickered in his eyes. "So maybe this bomber isn't a serial bomber so much as a bomber for hire?"

"It wouldn't even have to be the same client. It could have been four different clients. Maybe he's out there, swimming in the muck of society's underbelly, looking for clients just like a hit man or a fixer would."

"It *would* explain why the bombs are the same but the targets aren't connected," Scanlon admit ted. He shot her a look of admiration. "Good catch, Cooper."

Though pleased by his praise, she tried not to show it. It had been a long time since she was the rookie sucking up to the more experienced agent. "I'm going through the possible suspects police came up with before we flagged the cases. Maybe the connection is with the enemies, not the bomber."

They both fell silent, just looking at each other until the air between them felt as thick as molasses. Scanlon made the first move, crossing to the dresser to pull out a T-shirt and a pair of sweats. His tee, she noticed, was bright orange, emblazoned with the University of Texas logo.

He saw her smiling at the selection. "What?"

She put the knapsack on the end of the bed and pulled out the sleeping clothes she'd selected. "We're a pair, aren't we?"

His eyes darkened as he took a step toward her. Her muscles contracted, like an animal preparing for flight, which was strange, because the last thing she wanted to do was run away from the man moving toward her in slow, deliberate paces.

"You're going to want to close the bedroom door tonight," he said in a low voice that sent a ripple of fire shooting through her belly. "Might even want to lock it."

She didn't think he was warning her against intruders from outside. Lifting her chin, she leveled her gaze with his. "I'm not afraid. I can handle anything that happens."

She wasn't talking about intruders, either.

"I'm not sure I can." His voice came out in a hoarse whisper, and he backed away from her, the heated air between them replaced by the dank chill that had descended on the house with the fall of night.

She released a soft sigh of frustration as he slipped out of the bedroom and closed the door behind him.

SCANLON DIDN'T LIKE LEAVING Isabel back at the cabin while he ventured into town the next morning, but he couldn't avoid Bolen Bluff forever. He had to go for supplies, for one thing. Isabel might pretend she was feeling better, but ketamine could take a big physical toll, and he needed to be sure he had plenty of healthy food, water and painkillers on hand.

He could drive over to Mentone or all the way into Fort Payne, he supposed, but that would be avoiding the inevitable. He was here to insinuate himself into the very fabric of life in the insular little hamlet. It was time to get back to the job he'd come here to do.

Bolen Bluff was little more than a cluster of storefronts lining Poplar Street, on which no poplars grew at all, only scrubby oaks, hickories and pines. Most of the people in town either worked right here in the area or lived on welfare while they grew marijuana and cooked methamphetamine with stolen or illegally procured pseudoephedrine. The pot growers and meth cookers were all affiliated with the Swains in some way, of course. Anyone who tried to horn in on the Swains' business around Bolen Bluff ended up dead or missing.

It hadn't always been that way. When Scanlon had been little, Bolen Bluff was still a pretty little hamlet in the north Alabama hills, close enough to the Desoto National Forest to benefit from some of the tourism that usually centered around Fort Payne and the Little River Canyon.

But the Swains were starting to get a foothold even then. They were an old family, descended from the original settlers, if the stories were to be believed. Jasper Swain's own father had been a moonshiner, but the end of Prohibition had made home brew a losing proposition. The rise of marijuana as the drug of choice in the fifties and sixties, however, had given the Swain family a new source of income.

Meth had come next, easily made during the days when a person could actually buy pseudoephedrine products right off the shelves of any pharmacy. Crackdowns on meth production had driven those products behind the pharmacy counter in recent years, but there were still ways for resourceful criminals to get what they needed to cook their product.

Eventually, the criminal elements had driven out all but the most stubborn residents of Bolen Bluff, leaving only a few hardy souls to battle the Swains' complete takeover of the town.

The only grocery store in town belonged to one of the Bolen Bluff holdouts, Deanie Floyd, a sun-bronzed woman in her late sixties who was still pretty enough in her waning years to convince Scanlon that she'd been a knockout in her younger days. She flashed him a wary smile as he entered but greeted him politely enough from the manager's counter.

"How're you doing this beautiful day, Mr. Shipley?"

"I'm just fine, Mrs. Floyd. I'm in the mood for some fresh fruits and vegetables—what do you have today?"

She waved at the produce section. "Got a fresh load of broccoli and cauliflower this morning, and the strawberries and cherries are in prime shape. A little early for peaches, but they're not bad if you cook 'em. Plenty of good pears and apples." She gave him a quick look through narrowed eyes. "You thinkin' about cookin' that girl of yours something special?"

It took a quick, panicked second to realize she was talking about Dahlia McCoy and not Isabel. "That may be a little beyond my abilities, Mrs. Floyd. Just thought I'd have a few things available in case she wanted to get creative in the kitchen."

Deanie smiled. "You mean, you're hoping *she'll* cook *you* something special."

"You know all my secrets," he said aloud.

"Not yet," she said flatly. "But give me time."

Unease flushed through him as he turned and picked up a shopping basket. He had too damned many secrets that could blow up in his face any time as it was. Having to hide Isabel from the people of Bolen Bluff—both friends and foes—was going to be a nightmare.

Even as he gathered up food he knew she'd like, he started formulating a plan to convince her that the safest option for both of them was for her to go home to her family. They had the resources and the manpower to watch her back. If she wanted to keep looking at the files, she could do it from the safety of her own home. Anything she came up with, she could relay to Adam Brand.

As he was paying Deanie for the groceries, Davy McCoy and an unfamiliar man entered the store. They started to head straight toward the back when Davy caught sight of Scanlon. He gave a brief nod of recognition before following the other man down the aisle toward the far end of the grocery store.

"Hard to believe Davy McCoy and your Dahlia are related."

Scanlon nodded without making a comment.

"You ought to stay clear of Davy and the boys. They're nothin' but trouble."

Scanlon couldn't argue with Deanie about that. "I know how to keep my nose clean," he said, hoping the vague assurance would appease her.

"See that you do. It don't take long for a fellow to

get caught up in all that Swain mess around here. I've seen it happen often enough."

Scanlon just smiled and took the bag of groceries from the checkout stand. "Thanks a million, Mrs. Floyd."

She gave a little wave, her expression worried.

He'd just put the bag of groceries in the passenger seat of his truck and closed the door when a pair of soft hands covered his eyes. Dahlia's warm drawl asked, "Guess who?"

He felt a flutter of guilt as he pasted on a smile and answered, "The prettiest girl in Bolen Bluff."

"You are the sweetest thing." She dropped her hands and pulled him around to face her. "What're you doing in town this fine morning?"

"A little grocery shopping. Thought I'd also drop by the feed store, see what's shaking."

Her brow furrowed prettily. "You don't have any livestock to feed, which means you're just lookin' for trouble."

"I'm going to be fillin' in at the store during the barbecue on Saturday," he told her, wondering how she'd react.

She looked more surprised than alarmed by the information. "Who told you that?"

"Davy and Bobby came by yesterday. Said Addie herself had asked for me." He let a little hint of pride seep into his voice. To be asked to do anything by Addie was a big deal in Swain circles, since she was one of old Jasper Swain's proxies among the family. Maybe even the most notable one, since her other siblings didn't have much to do with the business. There was another brother, Albert, and sisters named Melinda and Opal, but none of them seemed to be part of the business now, though it had long been thought that Albert, at least, was involved at the time Jasper went to jail.

"Tell them no," Dahlia said.

"I can't do that. I've already said yes."

Dahlia looked ready to argue, but her gaze shifted to somewhere behind him, and her eyes narrowed.

Scanlon turned to see Addie Tolliver walking down the sidewalk toward the two of them, a smile on her handsome face.

She was a tall, rawboned woman in her early sixties, with a wide brow and freckled skin grown leathery from so many years in the hot Alabama sun. She was lean for a woman her age, and muscular, as if she'd done a lifetime's worth of hard work. Of course, in her case, the exercise had been harvesting marijuana and hauling their illegal wares from place to place rather than honest hard work and sweat.

She joined them next to Scanlon's battered Ford. "Davy and Bobby told me you're going to watch the store for me on Saturday. Kind of you to do so." She had a polite, almost formal way of speaking that gave her the air of a proper Southern lady. But the jeans and worn plaid shirt she wore over a ribbed tank top said anything but "proper Southern lady."

Scanlon sometimes wondered what the Swain family might have become had they chosen a legitimate way of life. They were an odd clan, with customs that nobody in the family had the guts to break. Or maybe they just lacked the desire to break with the customs. They took pride in being Swains, the same pride he'd feigned with Dahlia moments before.

"I'm happy to do it, Miss Addie." He could feel Dahlia's eyes on him, her displeasure palpable.

"I'll have the boys bring you a plate from the barbecue before you go," Addie said, then turned her gaze to Dahlia. "You have something you want to say, Dahlia May?"

Dahlia just shook her head and walked away, heading toward the small dress shop on the corner.

"You should choose your friends carefully around here, Mark Shipley," Addie said, her gaze still following Dahlia down the street. "So many ways to go wrong in a place like this."

"Yes ma'am," he said.

She turned her blue eyes back to him. "I have a stock run down to Albertville this morning, so I reckon I'd better take my leave now. You have a fine day, Mark Shipley."

He tipped his baseball cap to her and watched her stride away, back in the direction she'd come.

She'd come here to speak to him specifically, he thought, wondering if that meant he was a step closer to acceptance among the Swains.

If so, it was that much more vital that he talk Isabel into going back home to Gossamer Ridge. Because once he got his foot in the door of the Swain family racket, things would get a thousand times more dangerous in Bolen Bluff.

Chapter Seven

The ketamine had done a number on her. She was as weak as a kitten and sweating buckets as she forced her trembling arms through another rep of bicep curls.

If she was going to be any help to Scanlon, she'd need to have more than just her brain in fighting shape. She'd slacked off on her fitness routine since undergoing Cooper Security's grueling orientation training, finding it hard to get motivated to work out daily after Scanlon's death. He had been her workout partner for almost two years, their natural competitive streaks driving them to the gym even on days when neither of them felt like putting in the time on the machines.

Just eight more curls and she could stop for a second—

The front door of the cabin opened, sending her nerves rattling. When she didn't hear Scanlon's voice, calling out an assurance, she put down the dumbbells as quietly as she could and padded si-

lently to the closet, which she'd left open in case she needed to hide in a hurry.

She left the closet door open a crack, just enough space for her to press her eye to the opening and look out on a narrow slice of the bedroom.

She heard footsteps, faint at first as they moved around the front room. They grew louder as the intruder headed down the hallway and detoured into the bathroom.

As she looked toward the hallway, her gaze snagged on the portfolio sitting on the edge of Scanlon's dresser.

The one containing all the notes and evidence they'd gathered on the serial bombings.

Swallowing a profanity, she opened the closet and darted out into the room, her hand on the Beretta holstered on her hip. She grabbed the portfolio and scooted back to the closet, barely drawing the door to before the footsteps coming down the hall entered the bedroom.

Her pulse thundered in her ears, nearly eclipsing the sound of the man's thick boots on the hardwood floor. She caught just a glimpse of him as he passed through the slim strip of room visible from her position, her breath hitching as a flash of memory flooded her brain.

Blue eyes, clear and hard. Gazing down at her, crinkled with a mean smile.

He'd been one of the men. The one she'd thought, for a brief time, was Jasper Swain.

He was a lot younger than old Jasper was now, but he looked remarkably like the younger photos of the man. Same sandy red hair and cobalt eyes, same rangy build and freckled complexion.

This one was definitely a Swain. But she had gathered photos of all the Swain family operatives in conjunction with her research, and this man was not among them.

Could he be the man her brother mentioned? The J. T. Swain who'd worked for MacLear as a Special Services Unit operative?

The intruder took his time, walking slowly around Scanlon's bedroom as if he owned the place. Hearing drawers slide open and shut, Isabel clutched the portfolio to her chest and sent up a quick prayer of thanks that she'd seen the file in time to retrieve it.

Would he search inside the closets? What was this guy looking for? Did he suspect Scanlon was a plant?

Her pounding pulse notched higher when she heard the front door open again. Aware that if the new arrival was Scanlon, he might well call out her name to let her know he was there, she held her breath in terror.

But all she heard was the sound of footsteps walking slowly down the hallway. Another intruder?

She heard a soft scraping sound inside the bedroom, and it was all she could do to remain still, her curiosity nearly overcoming her.

The footsteps coming down the hall entered the room. She peered through the space in the door and saw Scanlon walking slowly toward the far side of the small room.

His footsteps stopped for a minute, then he spoke. "You can come out. He's gone."

Isabel's legs trembled as she pushed to her feet and exited the bedroom closet. She spotted Scanlon at the window, gazing through the narrow space between the curtain panels.

"How did you know someone was in here?"

"I set a trap at the front door." He showed her a piece of narrow filament. "If the door opens, it breaks this. It was broken when I arrived."

"How did you know I didn't go out the door myself?"

He looked at her. "Because you're too smart to stick your head out of this house with people looking for you."

She nodded toward the window. "Do you know who that is?"

He shook his head. "I didn't get a look at his face, but he doesn't look like anyone I've ever seen around here."

"He's a Swain, for sure," she said flatly. "I got a look at his face when he came into the room." At Scanlon's arched eyebrow, she added. "I left the closet door open a crack."

"What makes you think he's a Swain?"

She described the man to him. "I'm nearly positive he was one of the men who tried to abduct me. He was the one with the blue eyes. For a second, I thought he was old Jasper Swain himself. He looks a lot like the old man."

He looked down at the portfolio she still held clutched against her chest. His brow furrowed. "You're still studying those files?"

"Yes, but I took a break," she admitted, glancing toward the array of dumbbells she'd been using to work out. "I was trying to get some strength work in."

He glanced at the dumbbells and back at her. "Thank God you remembered to grab the file when you hid in the closet."

"I didn't, at first." She tamped down a shudder at the memory of her close call. "I ran out and got it just before he came into the bedroom."

"Oh, Cooper." He wrapped his hand around the back of her neck and pulled her to him, sliding his arm around her shoulder to hold her close. She leaned her head against the curve of his neck, wishing they could both go back six months to a time when not everything they did or said could get them killed.

"What if the guy who was just in here is J. T. Swain?" she asked, pushing aside her futile wish. "He could be a distant cousin with the same name or something like that."

Scanlon's fingers played in her hair. "I guess it's

possible. I'd feel a lot better if I could figure out where J. T. Swain figured into the family."

"I know. I went through the 'who's who' portion of the files this morning before I started working out. There are photographs of every Swain and Swain clan operative we know about in that file, and this guy definitely wasn't one of them."

Scanlon turned toward her, cradling her face between his big palms. His gaze was electric, sending an answering shock through her system, flooding her body with heat. Could he hear the way her pulse roared in her ears? Did he have any idea what he could do to her with a mere touch?

She knew he wanted to kiss her. Saw it in the way his gaze dipped to her lips, his own mouth parting on a shaky breath.

But whatever he might have wanted, what he said was, "It's time for you to go."

She stared at him for a moment, certain she had misunderstood. But the stubborn set of his jaw and the way he slanted his gaze away from her told her she was hearing things just fine.

She pulled away from his grasp, turning her back on him. She clutched the portfolio more tightly to her chest. "No."

"You can take the files with you. Brand can get me a second set. You can do everything at home that you're doing here, and you'll be a hell of a lot safer doing it."

She whipped around to face him. "I'm getting in your way? Is that what you're saying?"

"People come here. Invited and uninvited. Having you here complicates things." He kept his voice low and hard, but she saw a telltale tremble in his jaw.

The worst part was, she didn't really have an argument in favor of her continued presence here, did she? There wasn't one good reason to stick around and make things harder for either one of them. She should just pack her things and get out of here the second Scanlon could arrange it.

"Fine," she said aloud.

His gaze flickered as if he were surprised by her easy acquiescence. He pressed his lips to a thin line and frowned. "Just like that?"

She sank onto the end of the bed. "You're right. My being here is a problem for you, and I don't want you to get killed because I'm being a big baby about being your partner again. You and Brand have something set up here, and the longer I stay, the more I'm screwing it up for you."

He sat next to her. "If they weren't after you, I'd bring you in on this in a heartbeat. I'd tell everyone you were my girl from back home in Texas." He gave her a nudge with his shoulder and smiled. "You can fake a twang, can't you?"

"With the best of them," she answered in a decent Texas accent. "How would you break it to Dahlia?" she added, even though she knew she was being pathetic now.

"I'd tell her you were my girl first," he said in a low, growly voice that scattered goose bumps across her back and arms. "I don't want you to go, Cooper. But you have to."

She leaned her head on his shoulder. "How long do you think you'll have to play this part?"

"Could be years."

She blinked back hot tears and rubbed her cheek against his arm. "Try to make it months. Okay?"

"Okay—"

A phone rang nearby, loud and jarring. There was a landline hooked up next to the bed. Isabel had figured it was there only for show, since most of the phone calls Scanlon would need to make were done on the satellite phone.

Scanlon eyed the phone as if it had morphed into some sort of alien creature. "Only the Swains know that number." He crossed to answer the ringing phone. "Hello?"

He listened for a second, then slanted a quick look at her. "Yeah, okay. That'd be cool." His voice came out easy and unguarded, but his expression was tense and troubled.

Isabel edged closer, trying to figure out what was going on at the other end of the line. She could hear only the faintest buzz of a voice. A male voice, she thought.

"I'll be there," Scanlon said. "Thanks for asking." He hung up the phone and looked at Isabel. "We'll have to postpone any attempt to spirit you out of here at least another day," he said, still frowning.

"Who was on the phone?"

"Davy McCoy. He and a couple of the Swains are going coyote hunting tonight around six and want me to go with them."

She didn't like the sound of that idea at all. "You're going out with Swains carrying guns? Have you lost your mind?"

"That's why I'm here in Bolen Bluff, Cooper. I'm trying to get in good with the Swains so they'll let me in on what they're really up to around here."

"They're up to cooking crack and growing weed," she shot back, shaking her head.

"And blowing things up."

"If they're even connected to those bombings."

"Those bombs are Jasper Swain specials, right down to the shrapnel they pack in there."

"Needles and nails," she murmured. She knew the files backward and forward by now.

"And gasoline-soaked cotton packing," Scanlon added. "They're connected. And if you're right about their going into the 'bomb for hire' business, they could take a new job at any minute. I have to make sure that doesn't happen. It was only fool luck that kept that fire at the movie theater in Mississippi from spreading to the homes nearby. A lot of innocent people could have been killed."

He was right. She knew he was right. It just didn't make it any easier for her to let him walk out that

door in a few hours with a bunch of animals a lot more deadly than the coyotes they'd be hunting.

He caught her hand and gave it a squeeze. "Let's forget about it for a few hours. Come on." He tugged her hand. "I bought you a surprise."

She dropped the folder on the end of the bed and followed him into the kitchen, where a large sack of groceries sat on the rickety card table.

"Dig in," he said, standing back.

She rifled through the bag, excited to find fresh fruits and vegetables inside, along with a small box of cream cheese Danish pastries. She gave him a look. "You thought you'd be able to coax me into a better mood with Danishes?"

"It was worth a try."

She grinned. "You know me too well."

"You're going to have to do the cooking," he warned. "My culinary skills are equivalent to those of a college kid who's really good at dialing the pizza place for takeout."

"What have you been eating for six months?" she asked, as she picked out a bunch of asparagus and some green onions from the bag.

"Soup. Sandwiches. Sometimes together."

She rolled her eyes at him. "Some things never change."

"There's a nice piece of salmon at the bottom of that bag. The lady at the grocery store—Deanie Floyd—thinks I'm planning a special dinner for Dahlia."

Isabel's excitement waned a little. She set the wrapped piece of salmon on the kitchen table. "Maybe you should save this for her, then. If Deanie says anything to her—"

"Deanie doesn't talk to the Swains," Scanlon said flatly. "Or anyone connected to them. She just keeps her head down and tries to keep them from deciding she and her store aren't wanted in Bolen Bluff anymore."

"That's horrible. How can things like this still happen in this country?"

"Law enforcement has to pick their battles. The Halloran County sheriff is a cousin of the Swains, so things fall between the cracks."

"There was a time they didn't," Isabel said. "The sheriff who arrested Jasper Swain all those years ago had guts. He didn't let the Swains cow him."

"Fat lot of good it did him. He ended up shot down in his own driveway." Scanlon's reminder was blunt and strained. She darted a curious look at him and saw that he looked angry.

"But he got his man first," she replied. "That's something, isn't it?"

"It is." Scanlon's expression cleared, and he picked up the salmon. "And I bought this for *you,* not Dahlia. I know you love grilled salmon."

"No grill," she said quietly, trying to hide the rush of pleasure his words had given her. "I can broil it instead."

He opened one of the cabinets beneath the stove

and pulled out a broiler pan. "I'll be your helper—there's a cooking word for that, isn't there?"

"Sous-chef?"

"Exactly. I'll be your sous-chef. Order me around."

She grinned at him. "You're just asking for trouble now, Agent Scanlon." His wicked look in reply made her laugh. "Okay, first thing you can do is unwrap the fish while I start preparing the vegetables." She slid the wrapped fish across the table to him.

While they worked, she stole a quick glance at the clock on the wall above the table. Ten minutes after noon. In just under six hours, he'd be going hunting with the Swains.

It felt like minutes, not hours. Not nearly long enough.

How was she going to get through tonight, waiting for him to come home?

SCANLON WASN'T A BIG FISH eater, but he had to admit his partner could flat out cook a salmon. "Who taught you to cook?" he asked her over their late lunch of salmon, steamed asparagus and garlic toast.

"My dad," she said with a faint smile. "Mom left not long after my eighth birthday, so Dad had to do it all."

"You don't talk about your mom." He'd never pushed her to tell him any of the particulars of her family back home in Maybridge, mostly because he had his own family secrets he was keeping and didn't think it was fair to know hers when he didn't intend to share his own.

"I don't see her much anymore. She made the choice to leave us behind, and we've all dealt with that."

"I'm sorry."

"It's okay." As she often did when talking about something emotional, Isabel lifted her hand to touch the large gold locket that hung around her neck on a narrow chain. It was one of her favorite pieces of jewelry, he knew. She wore it most days, though she hadn't been wearing it when he rescued her the previous day. She must have found it in the knapsack the FBI agents dropped off at the barn.

"Your lucky charm," he murmured, nodding toward the necklace. "Was it in the stuff they retrieved from the hotel?"

She nodded, dropping her hand back to her lap. "In all the chaos, I almost forgot I'd left it there."

"Did your mom give it to you?"

She seemed startled by the question, her brow furrowing. "No. It was something that belonged to a friend. Her name was Annie. She and her family moved to Gossamer Ridge when we were both in high school. We clicked immediately and became best friends."

He could tell by her expression that this story wouldn't have a happy ending. "What happened to her?"

She met his sympathetic gaze not with sadness, as he expected, but a roiling rage that turned her brown eyes coal black. "Her house was bombed by some racist degenerates who couldn't deal with the fact that a white woman had married a black man. Annie's stepfather was black, and that's what got her killed. How sick and twisted is that?"

He reached across the table to touch her hand and found it trembling. "I'm sorry."

"It's one reason I started focusing on the serial bomber, you know?" She eased her hand away from him, raising it back to the locket. "I never told you that because I was afraid you'd think I was caught up in my own agenda rather than following the FBI's agenda."

He had no room to question her motives, given his own reasons for joining the FBI. "How'd you get the locket?"

"Her brother gave it to me. He said it was a favorite piece of hers, given to her by her grandmother. He said she loved it so much she never wore it because she was afraid the chain might slip and she'd lose it."

He nodded at the clasp. "What's inside it?"

"I don't know," she admitted. "The clasp is stuck, and I didn't want to risk breaking it by trying to pry it open."

"It must have been hard, losing people you loved

so young." He knew what that kind of loss felt like, too. He'd seen his father murdered right before his eyes.

If only he could remember how it happened.

"I can't arrange for your extraction before tomorrow now," he said.

She licked her lips, but her only other response was to poke at her half-eaten salmon fillet with her fork.

"You know why it's important that you go, right?"

She nodded, but her thinned lips weren't a good sign.

"I want you to be safe."

She looked up at him then, her dark eyes blazing. "You want me off your mind so you can go on with your operation. I get that. Having me around complicates everything."

"I want you to stay," he said baldly, unable to stop the words from coming out of his mouth.

"What we want doesn't matter." She put her fork down, giving up any pretense of eating. "I just don't—" She closed her eyes, as if she were in pain. "I don't know why it had to be you. You're not an undercover specialist."

He couldn't explain it to her without telling her everything he'd kept carefully hidden for decades. Even Adam Brand didn't know how deeply personal this assignment was to him. And maybe that was a bad thing—maybe he was too close to this whole mess to be objective and smart.

But this undercover operation might be the best chance he'd ever get to find out exactly which one of the Swains had killed his father over twenty-five years ago. He'd risk anything, sacrifice anything, to find the answer.

Anything but Isabel Cooper's life.

Chapter Eight

Scanlon had long suspected the coyote hunts the Swains liked to talk about rarely resulted in any dead coyotes. The wily creatures remained plentiful, roaming freely at night, as Scanlon had discovered on many of his furtive trips to the FBI drop site after dark. So far, Davy McCoy and the two Swain cousins had done little more than drink home brew from plastic water bottles, smoke a few joints and try to one-up each other on what badasses they were.

"You ever killed anyone?" Leamon Tolliver asked Scanlon as they crept through the woods with about as much stealth as a drunk trying to navigate a room full of wind chimes.

"Yeah." Scanlon knew his answer would ring true because it was. He'd killed a rapist who'd drawn down on him and Isabel while they were tracking him inside an abandoned office building in D.C. It had been a lucky shot—he'd never been much of a marksman. Isabel was a much better shot, but she'd had her back to the guy when he'd made his move.

She'd been directly in the man's line of fire, so Scanlon had aimed for the man's center mass. He'd hit him in his neck, but the bullet had done its job. "Shot the son of a bitch for lookin' at my girl the wrong way," he elaborated tersely.

"And got away with it?" Davy asked.

"Cops didn't care—guy I shot wasn't no Boy Scout, either."

"Let's go on down this way," suggested the third man, a Swain cousin named Dillon Creavey, son of Jasper Swain's cousin Del. After six months of getting to know the Swain clan, Scanlon practically had a family tree etched in his brain.

Which was why J. T. Swain's sudden appearance on the scene came as a surprise—and a worry.

They were heading toward the river, a good place for coyotes. Watering holes drew the small mammals coyotes preyed on. Scanlon clutched his borrowed rifle more tightly, hoping the coyotes would hear them coming. As far as he knew, the coyotes in these woods weren't making a nuisance of themselves with the local livestock, so he was in no hurry to shoot one.

Not that he'd be likely to hit it, he thought with a secret smile. He was even worse with a rifle than with a pistol.

"Well, look there," Leamon Tolliver said, as they came within sight of the river. "We have visitors."

Scanlon peered through the gloom ahead and spotted a tent set up about ten yards from the river's edge, glowing from some source of light within. He glanced at his companions and noticed that all three of them were looking at the campsite with slight smiles on their faces.

His stomach tightened. Was this a test? Was that why Leamon had asked him if he'd ever killed anyone?

Were they going to order him to kill these campers?

"RECKON THEY'VE REACHED the campsite." J.T.'s voice was a low drawl that reminded Opal of her brother Jasper in his prime.

J.T. looked like her side of the family, too, which was a blessing, because her late husband, Earl, hadn't been much in the looks department. Of course, she hadn't been a knockout herself, but what looked coarse and mannish on her looked manly in her son. "What do you think it'll prove about Mark Shipley?"

"Don't know," J.T. admitted. "If he's a fed, I reckon those fellows will be able to tell."

"What makes you leery of him in the first place?" Opal kept the question casual, not wanting to pique her son's curiosity too much. As proud of him as she was, she knew he wouldn't care to see her as a rival for power in the family.

She'd have to handle J.T. carefully.

"Ain't sure." J.T. looked out the kitchen window

at the inky night. "Feels like I ought to know who he is."

"You think you've seen him before?"

"I don't know." J.T. turned back to look at her. "Jasper's not gonna last forever. Jail's takin' a toll already, and he ain't that young to begin with."

"You want to head the family."

"I'm the only choice. Jasper Junior's in the ground, and Tammy don't want nothing to do with the family."

"Leamon might have somethin' to say about that," she said, leading him carefully.

"Leamon's an idiot," he spat. "He ain't no obstacle."

Opal hid a secret smile. J.T. was a dangerous man in many ways, but he wasn't unpredictable, at least not to his mother.

"What if your friends tell you Mark Shipley ain't a fed? You still gonna keep an eye on him?"

"I'll keep an eye on anyone who ain't family."

Like you're keeping an eye on the McCoys? Wild-eyed Davy and too-big-for-her-britches Dahlia were trouble. Even Opal, though staying on the edges of the family business for now, could see the McCoys would be a problem for the Swains, sooner or later.

The key was to figure out now how to make the coming storm work to her own advantage.

"WHAT ARE WE GOING TO DO here?" Scanlon asked Davy quietly, as they worked their way toward the tent. He noticed the other three weren't trying to be stealthy at all, which either meant they weren't going to try to ambush the people inside or they didn't give a damn if the people knew they were coming, because they were about to unleash a bullet-flying hell on earth that nobody could live through.

Two men came out of the tent and stood at the entrance, giving them long, wary stares as they approached to within five yards. The taller of the two was a dark-haired man in his late thirties. Broad shoulders, a muscular build and sharp gray eyes suggested he wouldn't be a pushover. Something about him seemed strangely familiar, though Scanlon didn't think he'd ever met the man before.

The shorter man was no slouch, either, making up for his lesser size with a powerful build and a jaw that jutted out like a hunk of granite, as if daring them to try anything. He had sandy blond hair that glimmered in the light from the Coleman lantern he held out in front of him to get a better look at the newcomers.

Neither man appeared to be carrying firearms, but they could easily have holsters tucked behind their backs.

"Hello," Davy called out, his voice disarmingly friendly.

"Hello," the dark-haired man said carefully. Definitely not a local; his accent pegged him as a Midwesterner. His companion just nodded at Scanlon and his companions.

"Y'all doing some fishing?" Leamon asked, grinning like a kid. Scanlon couldn't blame the sandy-haired man for shooting a look of alarm at Leamon. He was probably already hearing "Dueling Banjos" in his head and wondering how soon someone would tell him to squeal like a pig.

"Yes," the dark-haired man answered. "You?"

"Coyote hunting," Davy answered. "They're all up in these hills, bothering the livestock."

Scanlon noticed both of the men were looking at him. He met their gazes without flinching, but he was now more convinced than ever that Davy and the other two men had brought him out here to this tent on purpose. It was definitely a test.

But he no longer thought shooting these two men played into the scenario. On the contrary, if Scanlon's instincts were right, these two men were in on the plan. Davy, Leamon and Dillon wanted these two men to see Scanlon for some reason.

Did they already suspect he might be a fed?

Scanlon looked more closely at the two men, while trying to seem mostly uninterested. The blond-haired man was completely unfamiliar to him, but the dark-haired guy had set off a low-level alarm the second he'd laid eyes on him. He'd seen him before. In town? Back in D.C.?

He pushed back a lock of his own hair, which had been growing long for six months now. He'd deliberately cut back on his shaving these days, as well, letting his beard grow for days at a time before giving it a trim. He was dressed in ratty camouflage he'd picked up at a thrift store over in Guntersville when he'd learned that the Swains liked to go hunting. Even if this man had seen him before, back when he was Mr. Clean-cut FBI Agent, it wouldn't be easy to recognize him, especially in the low light.

"You fellows eaten anything?" the sandy-haired man asked. His accent was a broad Louisiana drawl. Scanlon wouldn't be surprised to learn he wrestled alligators for fun.

"Nothin' but a few crackers before I came out," Davy answered. "You offerin'?"

"Sure. We caught us a nice mess of bluegills out of the river earlier today. Fried 'em up over the fire and we're just about to start eating." The blond grinned at them. "You want some? There's plenty—don't want to have to throw it away."

"Sure would," Leamon said eagerly. Too eagerly. Now Scanlon was sure they were up to something.

So it was a test, he thought, as he followed the other three men into the spacious tent. Inside, two sleeping bags took up about half the space. The bags were high-end products, of a brand serious wilderness campers would use. Two expensive rifles leaned against the side of the tent near the sleeping bags. Across from there, a large plastic cooler sat in the corner, acting as a table. A plastic plate piled high with fried fish sat atop the cooler.

"I'm Norman Bayliss," the dark-haired man

said. He nodded to his smaller friend. "This is Jeff Munroe."

"I'm Leamon Tolliver," Leamon said, "and this here's my cousin Dillon Creavey. That's Davy McCoy and the quiet fellow over there is Mark Shipley."

Scanlon nodded in greeting. "Where're y'all from?" he asked, pleased with how nonchalant he sounded.

"I'm from Slidell, Louisiana," the one named Jeff answered.

"Mark here's from Houston," Davy said. "That ain't far from Louisiana, is it?"

"It's a little ways," Scanlon answered.

"I'm from Marion, Illinois, originally," Norman Bayliss said. "But we've both been living in Atlanta for the last few years. We both work at a construction company there."

Scanlon didn't buy that story for a second. He let his gaze linger on Norman Bayliss's face for a moment, then looked back at his companions. He found them all watching him rather than the two strangers.

He made a little face at them to let them know he found their stares odd. They all looked away quickly.

Good. Now he had them on the defensive.

He didn't look back at Bayliss again, instead turning his gaze around the large tent. "This is some fancy setup. Bet it cost you an arm and a leg."

"Got it at a military surplus store for next to nothing," Munroe said with a laugh. "You like to camp, Mr. Shipley?"

"Don't get much chance to," he answered lightly, letting his gaze move from Munroe to Bayliss. Bayliss's stance was oddly martial, almost as if he were standing at attention.

Almost as soon as he went into that stance, Bayliss relaxed it, but it was too late. Scanlon had seen it.

Suddenly he saw, with dazzling clarity, what this entire hunting trip was really all about.

These men were soldiers. The unconventional kind. That was why the dark-haired man seemed familiar to Scanlon—his face had been plastered on a list passed around to the FBI a couple of years ago when the MacLear Security scandal had first broken. His name wasn't Norman Bayliss. It was Nolan Alvarez, and he'd been one of the persons of interest the FBI had wanted to locate for questioning about the MacLear SSU.

No doubt Jeff Munroe was also a former SSU agent. And the Swain boys knew it. This silly coyote hunting trip had been aimed at bagging an entirely different prey.

He'd been trying to ease his way into the family's trust for months now. Before this invitation to go hunting, about the only thing he'd ever been invited to do with any of the Swains was watch the

store for Addie this coming Saturday while she and the family held their barbecue.

Was this one final test before letting him do that favor for the Swains? Bring him here and parade him in front of the big, bad soldiers of fortune?

It wasn't a bad plan, really, which made Scanlon wonder whose idea it had really been. Davy, Leamon and Dillon weren't the brightest bulbs on a family tree that didn't boast many bright bulbs at all. Someone else had probably come up with the notion—Addie, maybe. Or perhaps the SSU guys themselves. Either option would suggest a connection between the Swains and the rogue SSU operatives that he hadn't realized existed before.

Maybe it tied in, somehow, to the mysterious J. T. Swain?

Whoever had come up with the plan was smart enough to know that the MacLear SSU agents were uniquely suited to spot a fed. So much of the training, the mind-set and the habits of the MacLear agents would almost certainly echo that of the FBI, since most of MacLear's training personnel had been either former FBI Academy instructors or former military trainers.

They'd be able to spot the training tells better than just about anyone else.

Scanlon managed to school his features to a slack-jawed lack of interest in anything but the stack of tiny bluegill fillets that Jeff Munroe started passing around to the rest of them. Too bad for these guys that Scanlon wasn't a typical fed. Isabel's Academy training was as plain as the nose on her face, but Scanlon was damned near hopeless at tactical skills.

And now that he knew what these guys were looking for, he could make sure not to give the game away.

Davy pulled a couple of plastic bottles from his backpack. "Hooch," he said flatly, passing it to the guy calling himself Bayliss. "You might want to mix it with a little water. It's strong stuff if you're not used to it."

Scanlon took two crispy pieces of fish from the plate Leamon Tolliver passed to him. His stomach was in a knot, but he forced himself to eat the fish, and by the second bite, his hunger began to overcome his tension. He waved off the plastic cup of moonshine Bayliss offered and pulled his own plastic bottle from the pocket of his hip pack. It was diluted tea, which looked enough like homebrewed beer to pass. No way in hell would he risk getting liquored up with this bunch.

They stayed awhile longer. Davy, Leamon and Dillon had gone past buzzed and were headlong into blitzed by the time they took their leave and left the campsite.

"Reckon we're too pissed to hunt now," Davy said with a drunken laugh.

"Reckon so," Scanlon agreed. He felt the gazes of the two SSU agents on his back, but he didn't let himself stiffen up or turn around to see if they were still watching.

Apparently he'd passed the test, or they'd never have let him out of the tent alive.

ISABEL CHECKED THE SMALL alarm clock sitting beside Scanlon's bed. It was after ten—how long would Scanlon and the Swain boys hunt, anyway? All night? The silence in the house was becoming downright oppressive.

A few minutes later, the silence was shattered by a loud noise from the front of the house, a couple of thuds that seemed to come from just outside, then silence again.

She reached behind her back, where her Beretta sat heavily in its holster. She slipped the weapon out and checked the clip as quietly as she could.

She listened for further sounds but heard nothing for almost a minute.

Slipping off the bed, she stepped out of the slippers she'd put on her feet to ward off the mild chill that had descended with nightfall. The hardwood floor beneath her feet felt gritty and cold, but she pushed herself forward, pausing just outside the entrance to the front room, her back flattened against the wall.

She listened for more sounds, her body tense to the point of snapping.

Suddenly, a flurry of bangs hit the front door. Frantic and hard.

"Anybody in there! I need help!"

Isabel's heart seemed to settle somewhere in the middle of her throat, thumping wildly. She eased around the doorjamb into the front room, the dim gloom eased by only a small light Scanlon had left on over the stove.

Crouching low to stay out of the line of fire through the door or windows, she moved closer to the door.

"I need help!" The voice outside was male. Frantic. Not a local—the Southern accent was light and urbanized. Maybe someone from Birmingham or Atlanta, where city life had sharpened edges to their fluid drawls.

"My son's hurt! I think he might be bleeding out!" If the man outside was trying to trick her into showing herself, he was doing a damned good job of sounding convincing. Raw fear suffused the gravelly voice. "My phone's not getting a signal—I need your help. Please!"

She eased over to the window and darted a quick look through the tiny space in the curtains. She could just make out the edge of the front porch. There was a dark form lying there in a heap, and she could hear a soft, whimpering noise now. A hint of moonlight revealed something dark and wet trickling across the wooden slats of the porch.

Someone was hurt. Bleeding.

If she didn't do something to help these people, that person could die. But what if it were a trick?

After a long pause, she knew there was no other choice. She had to take the chance.

Keeping the Beretta in hand, she turned the latch and opened the front door.

Chapter Nine

The walk back to Canyon Rock, where Scanlon had met his companions earlier that evening, seemed to take forever. The hike was a series of drunken zigzags, Davy and the Swain clansmen alternating between singing profane versions of old country songs and scuffling until Scanlon was afraid they were going to shoot each other dead in the woods, leaving him to explain to Addie Tolliver how he'd let her boys kill each other.

Canyon Rock finally loomed into sight, and Scanlon sighed with relief. What happened once they parted ways was their problem. "Sorry we didn't find any coyotes to shoot," he said, edging away. "At least we got a fish fry out of it."

"Nice guys, those fellows." Davy was a happy drunk, grinning at Scanlon as if he'd just told Davy he'd won the lottery. "I didn't 'spect them to be such nice guys."

"Shut up, Davy!" Leamon caught Davy in a headlock and dragged him away. Leamon was not a happy drunk.

Dillon, the youngest, followed them off like a clumsy puppy, running circles around them as he tried to keep his cousin from getting too rough with their friend.

Scanlon was glad to see the back of them.

He started to head back toward the cabin, but curiosity began to nag the back of his mind. Those MacLear guys—had they really come here at the Swains' request just to give Scanlon the once-over? Or were they already in the area for another reason?

The hike back down to the river would take fifteen minutes, tops, without Davy and the others to hold him back. He knew how to be a lot quieter than the Swain boys had been, too. He was pretty sure he could get within a few yards of the tent without being seen or heard, since the last six months in Bolen Bluff had helped him recover some of the backwoods skills his father had taught him when he was a young boy.

He'd sure like to get a better idea what those mercs were doing in Halloran County and what their connection to the Swain family might be. Because whatever had brought the two groups together, it couldn't be good.

"DID HE LOSE CONSCIOUSNESS?" Isabel winced when she unwrapped the bandanna from the young boy's head and saw the bloody skin flap hanging from the side of the child's scalp. His name was Tommy, his father had told her. He'd fallen while they were hiking back to their camp that evening and he'd hit a rocky outcropping, tearing a wound in the side of his head.

"No, but he's not good with blood—makes him woozy." His father, Pete, looked a little green himself. Isabel had coaxed him into one of the kitchen chairs.

"Then you'll just have to close your eyes, Tommy," she said to the little boy, as she examined the bleeding wound. It looked superficial, actually, as if the rock he'd hit had merely sliced a flap of skin away from his head. "How old are you?"

"Eight," he said in a hitching voice.

"Oh, you're a big boy, then." She cleaned the area, wincing at Tommy's whimper, then used the tips of her gloved fingers to gently place the skin flap back into position. She carefully examined the condition of the skull beneath the wound to see if there were any signs of fracture. Tommy moaned a little more, but the bone felt firm under her touch.

"I think it looks a lot worse than it is," Isabel told Pete, flashing a quick smile. "I can bandage it up here to keep him from bleeding so much, but you'll need to get him to a doctor to make sure. Definitely going to have to have that stitched up, if nothing else."

"Thank you," Pete said, giving her a sheepish look. "I feel like an idiot for falling apart that way—"

"He's your son. Of course it freaked you out.

Do you have a way to get back to your vehicle?" she asked, securing the bandage around Tommy's wound.

"It's not that far," he admitted. "I just panicked when he started bleeding all over the place."

"Of course." Isabel crouched in front of Tommy. "Tommy, you're going to be okay. But your daddy's looking a little woozy himself, so he's going to need you to help him get back to the car without keeling over. You think you can do that?"

Tommy looked at her uncertainly.

"I bet you can," she said, looking him straight in his big brown eyes. "Because you're a hero. I can tell. Only a hero would have sat here and let me check him over this way without crying like a baby."

Tommy blinked at her, his lips curving a little in the middle of his blood-smeared face. "I didn't cry like a baby," he admitted.

"I sure could use your help, big guy," Pete said, catching on to Isabel's plan. He held out his hand to his son.

Tommy slid off the chair and crossed to take his father's hand. "Come on, Daddy. We better get you to the car."

Isabel walked them to the door. "I'm not sure where the nearest hospital is—"

"There's a clinic in town. I think they keep pretty late hours." Pete smiled at her. "I don't know what we'd have done without your help."

"I'm just glad I was here," she answered.

She didn't linger at the door, which she knew Pete might find rude. But she'd already taken enough chances tonight as it was. She stripped off her gloves and locked up behind her, pausing at the table to clean up the mess Tommy's bloody head wound had made.

By the time she'd hidden the evidence of her first aid in the trash can next to the refrigerator, the clock on the wall showed 10:45 p.m.

And still no sign of Scanlon.

How much more blood had spilled tonight in Halloran County?

GETTING CLOSE TO THE TENT by the river wasn't easy. The location had apparently been chosen with some care, as if the tent's inhabitants had wanted to make it difficult for anyone to stage an ambush.

These fellows were almost certainly former SSU agents. They knew better than to trust anyone, even partners in crime like the Swains.

Especially like the Swains.

But Scanlon was careful, too, keeping low, taking his time. He managed to get within ten yards of the tent without being observed, and there he settled down and searched his belt pack for the personal sound amplifier he'd picked up at a Fort Payne drugstore on an earlier supply run. He inserted the earpiece into his ear and found that the soft murmur of sound coming from within the tent turned into intelligible speech.

"Can't believe J.T. sent those rednecks on a job like this. What idiots." That was Munroe's voice, the Louisiana drawl as strong as ever.

"Can you believe they thought that Shipley guy was a fed?" That was the one named Nolan Alvarez, who'd called himself Norman Bayliss. His tone suggested utter contempt. "I mean, feds are usually dolts, but this guy makes even the worst feds I know look like superheroes."

Thank you very much, Scanlon thought with a grin. He'd worked hard to look like a dolt. He supposed Alvarez forgot the other part of superhero stories—they all had alter egos. Hiding in plain sight was what superheroes did.

"Are you sure you can vouch for J.T.?" Alvarez asked.

"I thought so. He was pretty good in a skirmish." Munroe's voice came out like a shrug. "But if he's blood kin to those rocket scientists, maybe not."

"Well, better get some shut-eye. We're supposed to report to Kurasawa by nine tomorrow. We've got to be up and back to the truck by sunrise."

No, not yet! Scanlon grimaced with frustration as the Coleman lantern extinguished, plunging the tent into darkness. He'd learned only enough to raise a dozen more questions.

He waited a few minutes longer, until the sound amplifier picked up the snuffling noise of one of the men snoring. Taking as much care as he'd used to sneak down to the tent, he made his way back up the side of the mountain and headed east to his cabin near the mountain crest.

Kurasawa, he silently repeated several times, hoping the name would mean something to Adam Brand when he called in the report. And the former SSU agent named J. T. Swain was definitely kin to the Swains here in Bolen Bluff—also useful information.

The thick palisade of trees thinned out at the edge of the clearing where his cabin sat. He saw a faint light glowing inside, where he'd left the bulb on over the stove. Otherwise, the cabin looked quiet and still.

He climbed the wooden steps in a hurry, almost losing his footing when his boot hit a slick patch at the top. Pausing, he pulled the penlight from his belt pack and shined it down at the top of the porch.

A large crimson stain gleamed in the narrow beam of light.

His stomach lurching downward, he crouched and touched his fingertip to the spot. The liquid was slightly viscous, adding to his growing conviction that he was looking at a small pool of blood. One sniff and he knew for sure. There was no mistaking the iron-rich odor of fresh blood.

He scanned the rest of the porch with the penlight and saw the faint evidence of muddy footprints on the wooden slats by the door. Blood drops moved toward the door.

Or did they move away from the door instead?

He walked quietly to the door, heel to toe to limit the noise. With a flash of penlight, he saw that the filament he'd left in place on the door was broken in two.

Please, God, please—

He found the door locked, but that was no surprise—it had been locked earlier when the man he believed to be J. T. Swain had gotten inside the cabin. Hell, for all he knew, the Swains owned duplicate keys for every house on this mountain.

He eased inside, the door making only the slightest noise. Enough to make Isabel hide, if she was still there.

Please still be here, Cooper. Please be alive. Please be all right—

Slowly, deliberately, he went room by room, looking for signs of a struggle. For blood. For broken furniture.

For a body.

He didn't see any blood, although the chairs in the kitchen were arranged differently from when he'd left. Isabel might have come into the kitchen for a quick snack, although he'd warned her to stick to the back of the cabin, where she'd have a better chance of reaching the closet in time to hide.

No signs of anything out of place—in fact, the bathroom was cleaner than he'd ever remembered it being.

He didn't know if that was a good thing or a bad thing.

Finally, his pulse rushing in his ears like white water, he entered the bedroom, trembling with dread. The room was empty and still, the closet door closed.

He walked slowly, softly, to the closet and stared at the doorknob. One turn, and he'd know whether or not she was still in the cabin.

One turn, and he might discover his worst nightmare had come true.

He closed his hand over the knob, took a deep breath, and turned it, yanking the door open.

And came face to face with the barrel of Isabel's Beretta.

"Son of a bitch!" Isabel hissed, pulling the weapon back and lowering her head to her chest. "You scared the hell out of me—I didn't even hear you coming until the front door opened."

He reached down and hauled her to her feet, looking her over for signs of injury. "Are you okay?"

"I'm fine. Scared out of my wits, but fine—" Her eyes widened. "Oh my God, you saw the blood on the porch."

"Hell, yes, I saw the blood on the porch—where did it come from?" He released her, his hands still shaking.

"It was a kid and his father—the kid had slipped and cut his head on a rock." Isabel holstered the Beretta and shoved a mass of dark curls away from her face. "It was a mess—kind of a partial scalping.

This whole flap of skin was flayed away from his skull—"

"Did they see you?" he asked, alarmed.

"I had to let them in," she admitted with a worried frown. "The man was freaking out completely, and I didn't know if the kid was going into shock or something—"

He wanted to argue, to chastise her for taking such a chance with her own life, but the truth was, she wouldn't be Isabel Cooper if she wasn't willing to put her life on the line to help a person in trouble.

He made himself calm down. Losing his mind wouldn't help a damned thing. "Did you tell them your name?"

She shook her head. "I got their names, though. The father was Pete. The little boy was Tommy. The man was about five-ten or five-eleven, with sandy brown hair. Brown eyes. Some graying at the temples. I'd say he's in his mid- to late thirties. The little boy had blond hair and brown eyes. Eight years old. They were Southerners, but their accents were mild—city folk. Their clothes and gear looked new and moderately expensive."

She rattled off the facts to him with the practice of an FBI agent trained to notice those kinds of things. Somehow, her professional calm seemed to seep into his bones, helping him regain a sense of perspective.

"Was the boy badly hurt?"

"It looked worse than it was. Head wounds bleed

a lot, which is what scared his daddy so much, but the wound itself was mostly superficial. It's going to require quite a few stitches, but he didn't seem to suffer a concussion or any kind of closed head injury."

"Good. How did they get up here?"

"Apparently they were hiking nearby when Tommy stumbled into the rock outcropping." She touched his arm. "I'm sorry. I know it was a huge risk to let them in—"

"You did what you had to," he said, meaning it. "Was he going to take his son to a doctor?"

"He said there's a clinic in town that's open twenty-four hours."

Scanlon's heart sank. "And it's run by a Swain cousin."

Isabel's eyes widened. "Oh, no."

"It's not likely he wouldn't mention getting help from a woman in a mountain cabin." Scanlon's mind raced as he tried to catalog all the ways Isabel's kindness could come back to bite them in the backside. "I think we have to assume that they'll start wondering who that woman could be."

"And they know you have a cabin on the mountain." Isabel looked ill.

"So we have to assume they'll be asking me some questions about the woman in my cabin."

"Tell them I'm your cousin," Isabel suggested quickly. "I came here because my creep of a hus-

Her lips thinned at his mention of home. "How do you know they didn't see through your cover?"

"Because I went back to spy on them after I parted ways with Davy and the others," he answered.

"You what?" She sounded horrified.

"I was careful. And I had this." He showed her the sound amplifier in his belt pack. "Unfortunately, they decided to get some sleep and bugged out on me before I could find out anything more. But they did confirm that J. T. Swain from the SSU is related to the Bolen Bluff Swains."

"So the SSU is working with the Swains?"

"Looks like it. I don't believe these guys think very much of the Swains—definitely not Davy and the boys who went out there tonight. Which makes me wonder what they're getting out of this collaboration."

"Maybe the Swains have something the SSU wants."

"We're assuming the SSU is some kind of cohesive unit. For all we know, they've scattered to the wind and they're taking jobs as they come, on an individual basis."

"It's not that simple," Isabel disagreed. "Last month, at least a dozen of them worked together trying to kill my sister-in-law. They're staying in touch."

"Paid for by that guy in Kaziristan—"

"Khalid Mazir," she supplied. "But we've been

looking into Mazir, and it turns out that he had some ties to Barton Reid. Reid had been pushing the U.S. to support Mazir's bid just before his arrest, which makes me wonder what Reid was going to get out of the deal."

Scanlon rubbed his gritty eyes. Every question he answered seemed to raise another question. "I can't imagine what Barton Reid could want from people like the Swains."

"If J. T. Swain is the connection—and I'm guessing he must be—maybe it has to do with the serial bombings."

He looked at her, not following.

"The SSU took a murder-for-hire job from Khalid Mazir, right? And we've been theorizing that the serial bomber may be taking these bombing jobs for pay, as well."

"And they started about the time all hell broke loose at MacLear," he added, pieces beginning to click into place. "He could have learned how to build a bomb at old Jasper's feet."

"Which would explain the similarity in the old bombs and the newer ones. Probably uses the same materials, same construction—old school."

"Swains do appreciate their own history," he agreed.

"I guess we can call it in to Brand in the morning—" She stopped short, and he saw in her stricken expression that she'd forgotten for a moment that she'd be leaving the next day, as well, if all went as planned.

He had forgotten, too, so caught up in the spirited back-and-forth that had characterized his partnership with Isabel Cooper. Watching her walk away again, even though he knew it was safer for everyone, was going to hurt, like pulling a scab off an old wound. "We should get some sleep," he said softly. "Been a long day for both of us."

She caught his hand as he rose to go. "When I thought you were dead, I used to talk to your ghost. You haunted me. Every day. But it was comforting, too, seeing you everywhere I looked."

"I'm sorry." He didn't know what else to say.

She rose to face him, lifting both hands to his face. She brushed her thumb across his mouth. "You could be at this assignment for a long time. The ultimate long con."

He smiled, enjoying the sensuous slide of the soft pad of her thumb over his lips. "Could be. Unless I catch a break and find Swain in the middle of building another bomb."

"I won't be able to see you. Or know if you're safe." She closed her eyes, her fingers dancing across his jaw line in light caresses, sending shudders of need rattling up his spine.

"Brand will let you know if something happens to me," he answered, moving his hands to her waist. She was fiery hot, burning his fingers through the thin cotton T-shirt she wore. He let his left hand drift upward, his fingers tracing over the curve of her rib cage until the back of his hand brushed the underside of her breast.

Her eyes fluttered open, black as midnight. Suddenly, she surged upward, her mouth hard and hot against his, driving him backward onto the bed.

Chapter Ten

She was out of control. A rush of emotions flooded her chest—fear, need, anger, joy, desire—and flowed through her into the hands that moved with fierce determination across his flat belly, pushing up the T-shirt he wore beneath his flannel shirt until her fingers tangled in the crisp, dark hair of his chest. Bending her head, she kissed the center of his sternum, feeling his heart pounding against her lips.

His fingers caught in her hair, drawing her up to face him. "We can't do this. You know we can't." He was trying to sound tough and logical, but she knew even better than he did how out of character it was for him to try to be the voice of reason.

That was her job in the partnership, keeping his flights of intuitive fancy from soaring too close to the sun. Of course, she wasn't doing much grounding at the moment, was she?

"I don't know anything anymore," she admitted, kissing his stubbled jaw. "I just know that if I have to leave you tomorrow, I don't want to leave anything unsaid or unfelt."

"You don't need to say anything." His voice came out in the faintest of whispers. "But neither of us is thinking clearly at the moment, and that's not a good thing—"

To her dismay, he eased her off him and stood up, moving toward the door without even looking at her.

"Scanlon—"

He stopped in the doorway but didn't turn. "Please don't make this more difficult."

"I don't think it can get more difficult than what you put me through already," she said, frustration making her unleash a little of the pent-up anger she felt. "You let me think you were dead for six long months. And that the bomb that killed you was really meant for me. So don't try to pretend anything that happens now will be more difficult than that. Don't you dare."

"There was no other way—"

"You could have trusted me."

He turned around then, his blue eyes blazing. "And you'd have been right in the middle of everything, trying to help me. Just like you are now."

"You know what I've realized?" she asked. "We're not nearly as good when we work apart. Don't you think there's a reason why you've been here six months and made only a little headway into infiltrating the Swains?"

"Why's that?" His voice was faint with annoyance, but she could tell he knew she was right.

"Because we are so much more together than we can ever be apart." She crossed to where he stood and caught his hands in hers. "I ground you so you don't go too far afield. You challenge me so I don't become hidebound by logic and rules. Alone, we try to play both roles, but we're no good at it."

He closed his eyes and bent his head until their foreheads touched. "I want you here, Cooper. And, God forgive me, if the Swains weren't after you, I'd keep you here with me."

Tears burned her eyes, but she blinked them back. "I'm willing to take the risk."

"I'm not." He pulled back, letting go of her hands. "I need to wash that blood off the porch before anyone else sees it. With some luck, nobody at the clinic will mention what happened tonight to any of the Swains." He turned to leave, not reacting this time when she called his name.

She sank onto the end of the bed, struggling with the tears that just wouldn't leave her be.

Logic told her he was absolutely right, and she had always been the kind of person who turned to logic first for the answers she sought. If she stuck around, not only was she putting her own life in danger but she was making it that much more difficult for Scanlon to pass himself off as Mark Shipley, the disabled vet who wouldn't mind getting involved in something illegal if it meant he could make some fast cash.

But if Scanlon had taught her anything over the

last few years, it was that logic wasn't the only way to look at a problem. Intuition could be valuable, as well.

And her intuition said there was more going on here than just a backwoods family of meth dealers. Scanlon was in more danger than he seemed to realize. She knew it, bone deep. And the thought of leaving him behind, with nobody but Adam Brand, in his big office hundreds of miles away, to watch his back, was a nightmare scenario she couldn't allow to happen.

SCANLON HAD HOPED FOR a little luck regarding Isabel's visitors the night before. But the minute he stepped inside the Bolen Bluff Urgent Care Clinic, his hopes were dashed by Davy McCoy's nasal drawl. "What's this about a girl at your cabin?"

Scanlon found Davy sitting a few feet away, holding an ice pack on his left wrist. Scanlon ignored Davy's question and nodded toward the man's wrist, which looked as if it had swollen to twice its normal size. "What did you do to yourself?"

"Dillon Creavey pushed me into a gully on the way back home last night. Said he was just kiddin'—like hell! I guess I was blitzed, 'cause I didn't realize 'til this morning how bad it hurt, so I came to get Doc Canning to take a look." Davy grimaced. "She's busy right now, but she gave me an ice pack for my wrist—said it might help with the pain and swelling."

"Nice of her," Scanlon commented.

"She said some guy and his kid had an accident up in the woods near your cabin, and some woman helped them out." Davy's expression was more salacious than suspicious, Scanlon noted, but that didn't mean some of the other Swains wouldn't find the story more troubling. "Someone in your cabin."

"My cousin," Scanlon said. "Just getting out of a bad marriage, and her ex is the rough sort, so she asked if she could stay for a night before she headed out of town. Said she didn't feel safe in a motel."

"Bet she had the scare of her life, then, with a couple of strangers showing up on her doorstep."

Scanlon managed a laugh. "Nearly peed her pants." Over Davy's bark of laughter, he added, "I guess she's tougher than she looks, though, 'cause she said she handled it just fine."

"Doc Canning said she did a good job bandaging the kid up. But you should have told us you had a girl up there." The humor in Davy's voice faded as if he'd finally remembered that Scanlon was still on probation with the Swains. "You know Addie and the boys like to know when strangers are around."

"I didn't know she was coming—she just showed up. And she's already gone, so there's nothing to talk about."

"She must've been mad when you hied off hunting while she was there. Leaving her alone and all."

"Reckon she was glad to be alone for a while.

Apparently her creep husband never let her have a minute to herself."

Davy nodded. "Well, okay. I'll tell Dahlia she ain't got nothing to worry about, then."

"Dahlia knows?"

"She's the one that brought me here, since I can't drive real well with my wrist all swollen up like a watermelon."

"Where is she now?" Dahlia was the jealous type—he couldn't be sure she wasn't headed up to the cabin right now.

"She said she had to go on to work—said I could call Dillon Creavey to come pick me up here since he was the jackass who knocked me into the gully in the first place." Davy eyed Scanlon. "What are you doing here?"

"My hand's been hurting me," Scanlon lied, rubbing the scar on his left hand. "Just thought I'd get it checked out, make sure there's not some more nerve damage going on. But it's not even hurting me right now. Maybe it was just one of those phantom pains people talk about."

"Bet that's it," Davy said with a nod. "Say, reckon you could give me a ride back to my place when Doc Canning's done?"

Scanlon needed to get back to the cabin and try again to get Adam Brand on the satellite phone to arrange Isabel's extraction, especially now that the Swains had an inkling she was here. He'd given the SAC a call earlier, but Brand hadn't answered the phone. But he couldn't say no, not without raising Davy's suspicions. "Sure."

Lori Canning came out of the back, talking to an older woman who was walking with a cane. The doctor was a pretty woman in her early thirties, with dark red hair and green eyes. There was enough resemblance to the Swains to tell she was related, but as far as Scanlon knew, she didn't want anything to do with the family business.

She nodded to Scanlon. "Heard y'all had a little excitement up on the ridge."

"Yeah, I hear my cousin's a real Florence Nightingale."

"Did a good job wrapping up Tommy Brubaker's head," Lori said with a smile. "If she'd like to volunteer here at the clinic sometimes, I'd be glad to have her."

"She's halfway to Nashville by now," Scanlon lied. "But next time I talk to her, I'll tell her you said so."

"Y'all gonna jaw all day or am I gonna get an X-ray?" Davy complained.

Dr. Canning shot Scanlon an apologetic smile and took Davy back into the exam room area.

Knowing Davy would probably be back there for a little while, Scanlon walked outside and crossed the street to the service station facing the clinic, digging change from the pocket of his jeans. He stuck a couple of coins into the slot of the pay phone on the outside wall of the service station and dialed Dahlia's cell phone number.

After five rings, the call went to her voice mail.

Maybe she was screening, he thought, trying not to get worked up. He'd called her using the pay phone a couple of times before, so she should recognize the number. But she could already be in a meeting at her office and ignoring all calls.

Or she could be at his cabin, looking for the mysterious woman Lori Canning had told her about.

He couldn't leave now, not after promising Davy to give him a ride home. That would make him look more suspicious than ever. Plus piss off Davy at a time Scanlon was trying to worm his way into the Swains' circle of trust.

But if he didn't warn Isabel that danger was coming—

The satellite phone. It was in the lock box, but Isabel knew him well enough to guess the digital code that would open it. She'd probably try to answer it, knowing the caller on the other end of the line was likely to be Adam Brand. Isabel would love to tell her former SAC what she thought of his lies.

Scanlon dug for more change. He had enough for four more calls—would she figure out the combination in time?

THERE WAS A PHONE RINGING in the house somewhere, the tone so muted that it had taken a couple of rings for Isabel to figure out what she was hearing.

Scooping up the folder of notes she'd been perusing, she ventured from Scanlon's bedroom into the hallway. The ringing sound was louder closest to the hall closet.

The satellite phone was ringing.

Had to be Adam Brand calling Scanlon—should she answer?

An image of her former SAC's face, so gentle and sympathetic as he comforted her the day he delivered the news of Scanlon's death filled her mind.

Smarmy, lying bastard.

She opened the closet and pried up the floorboard, sitting back on her heels in frustration when she saw that the phone was locked up in its metal box. A four-digit lock code on the lid of the box glared up at her in challenge.

The phone stopped ringing, and she stared at the digital code. "Guess you win this time," she murmured.

Then the phone started ringing again.

She grabbed the box up and stared at the code. What would Scanlon use for the code? Not his birthday or the last four digits of his Social Security number—that would be too obvious. It would be something personal to him, something almost nobody else would know about.

She thought a second, and remembered a running joke between them, something he called her when he wanted to drive her crazy.

On a hunch, she punched in the number 4-9-9-9. *Izzy.*

The lock clicked open.

She grabbed the phone before it stopped ringing again. "Yes?"

"I knew you'd figure out the code." Scanlon's voice greeted her on the other end of the line, startling her. He seemed to be calling from somewhere outside, light traffic noise competing with his low tone.

"Is something wrong?"

"Dahlia knows you're at the cabin. Or at least, she knows some woman is at the cabin. Dr. Canning told her in passing. Look, I've tried calling her cell but she's not answering. Be on guard—she's jealous. She might come looking for you. I can't talk any longer—I'm on my way back as soon as I can get there." He hung up the phone, leaving her rattled.

Okay, Dahlia knew there was a woman at Scanlon's place, and she was the jealous type. What were the odds she'd actually come here to try to confront the woman?

Pretty good, she decided, jumping into action. Hiding in the closet was the standard operating procedure around here when intruders showed up, but Isabel didn't think a closet would stop Dahlia McCoy. It might even be the first place she'd look, to see if there were women's clothes in the closet with Scanlon's. The hall closet, with its three rows of shelves, was entirely too small to accommodate a grown woman.

She was going to have to hide outside somewhere.

The first step she took was to open the bedroom window, just far enough that she could slip outside easily enough. She also kept the satellite phone on her, sliding it into the front pocket of her jeans.

In the bedroom closet, she found a dark camouflage backpack she'd noticed when she had hidden there before. She packed the portfolio of notes on the case into the backpack—she didn't want those notes to leave her sight for a minute—and added the contents of her clothing and personal items from the knapsack the FBI had delivered a couple of days earlier. No point in leaving evidence behind for Dahlia to find.

The last thing she checked was her Beretta. The clip was full—she'd never had a chance to use it back at the hotel, so all the ammunition was still there. She chambered a round, though she couldn't imagine any circumstance where she'd have to shoot Dahlia McCoy, and sat on the end of the bed to wait.

She didn't have to wait long. First she heard the sound of an automobile driving up the soft dirt track to the cabin, followed by the faint thuds of footsteps on the front porch. Within seconds, a soft rattling noise drifted back to the bedroom, the metal-on-metal clicks of a key in the lock.

She had a key to his house already?

Isabel padded quietly to the bedroom window and heaved first the backpack, then herself, outside, landing lightly in the clump of high grass next to the wall of the house. Closing the window until only a slim crack of space remained between the window and the sill, she crouched in the grass and scanned the woods behind her for any sign of movement. Except for the faint sound of new leaves rustling in the light April breeze, she heard and saw nothing.

Keeping her eyes on the woods, she focused her ears on what was happening inside Scanlon's house.

She heard footsteps clicking on the hardwood floors in Scanlon's bedroom, unsurprised that Dahlia McCoy would start there in her search for the other woman in Scanlon's life. She'd find nothing—thanks to Scanlon's heads-up, Isabel had time to erase herself from the cabin.

Before the end of the day, she realized with a sinking heart, she'd be erased permanently, on her way back home to Gossamer Ridge, with a bunch of new regrets to replace the old ones.

"I know you're here." Dahlia's deceptively sweet voice carried through the narrow gap in the window. "That tourist saw you. I know you helped his son— very noble. I'm not here to scratch your eyes out or anything trashy like that. I'd just like to know what I'm up against."

Isabel arched her eyebrows. She wasn't sure she entirely believed Dahlia's reassurances. Could be a trick to get the other woman into range of her claws.

Inside the room, she heard the *snick* of the closet door opening, and smiled at her foresight. Suspicious women always went for the bedroom closet.

She dared a quick peek. The intruder was tall and blond, just as she'd suspected. As Dahlia turned away from the closet, Isabel got a quick look at her face, just before ducking back out of sight. Pretty, too. Scanlon's usual type.

A new sound drifted toward Isabel, coming from somewhere down the mountain. A vehicle engine, the sound rough and familiar. Scanlon's old Ford pickup truck.

She flattened herself against the house to be sure nobody could see her from the dirt clearing that served as Scanlon's parking area. The nose of the Ford pickup came into view, barely, around the corner of the house. The engine cut and the door creaked open.

Bootfalls rang on the porch, loud enough that Dahlia surely heard him coming. Sure enough, Dahlia's heels clicked quickly toward the front of the house. Scanlon's voice boomed from the front room a moment later, loud enough that Isabel could hear it from outside.

"What the hell do you think you're doing?"

Chapter Eleven

Dahlia's answer to Scanlon's query was too faint to discern, to Isabel's frustration. She wished she could sneak back into the bedroom to better hear the conversation, but she wasn't foolish. Better to wait and let Dahlia clear out. Scanlon would tell her whatever he thought she needed to know.

And that was the problem, she thought with a grimace. What would he edit out? She was getting a little tired of Scanlon calling the shots about what she could and couldn't know about his operation here in Bolen Bluff.

To her surprise, their voices came nearer, and within seconds, both Scanlon and Dahlia were in the bedroom, only a few feet from where she crouched below the window. She could hear their conversation perfectly now.

But did she want to? To what lengths would Scanlon have to go in order to appease his girlfriend?

"You've gotta get over your jealous streak, Dahlia. You broke into my house looking for a woman who ain't even here—"

"I know she's here. Lori told me she was quite the angel of mercy for some poor tourist whose son was injured. Is that the kind of woman you like?" Dahlia's voice had lowered to a purr. "Is she as pretty as I am?"

As much as she hated herself for it, Isabel wondered how Scanlon would answer.

"She's my cousin and she was in trouble. I gave her a place to stay last night, and now she's gone."

"Is that really true?"

"Do you trust me or not?"

"I don't know," Dahlia admitted. "I want to."

"I don't get what you see in me," Scanlon said doubtfully. "I got a bum hand. I barely make enough in government handouts to keep food on the table and gas in my truck. Why would a woman like you look twice at a loser like me?"

"You're the only man in this town who's not a Swain."

"That's flattering." Scanlon's voice was quiet, as if she'd hurt him. Isabel's gut tightened painfully.

"I'm sorry. This place is like poison. I don't know why you ever wanted to live here."

"It's quiet," he answered. "Simple."

Even though she knew that Scanlon's reasons for being here in Bolen Bluff were anything but simple, she found herself drawn in by the plaintive tone of his voice.

"Too quiet," Dahlia murmured.

"Look, we haven't said we're exclusive, have we?"

Isabel raised her eyebrows at Scanlon's question.

"I thought it was understood, or I wouldn't have wasted my time." Dahlia's voice came out haughty and tense.

"Well, it's not."

After a moment of dead silence, Dahlia spoke, her voice dark with anger. "Is that your way of saying we're done?"

Isabel held her breath, waiting for Scanlon's answer. While she knew that having a connection to the Swain clan was a benefit, she wasn't looking forward to hearing Scanlon groveling to get back in Dahlia's good graces.

But his answer was unexpected. "That's up to you, Dahlia. You willing to do this, no strings?"

Isabel winced. *Harsh, Scanlon.*

"I'll have to think about it," Dahlia said coolly. "Because you're right about one thing. I *can* do better."

Her heels clicked an angry cadence across the hardwood floors, slowly fading. The front door opened and slammed shut, and her footsteps echoed across the porch.

Isabel crouched low as she heard the soft purr of an engine start at the front of the house. She waited until the sound of the car had nearly died away before she unfolded her body, wincing at the aches and twinges.

"Cooper?" Scanlon's voice came from inside the room, barely more than a whisper.

Standing to look at him through the narrow gap between the window curtains, she tapped lightly on the windowpane. He whirled at the sound, his eyes widening.

She pushed the window upward. "Help me back inside."

He took the backpack she handed through the window and helped her onto the sill. "Why the hell did you go outside?"

"Because I knew she'd look in the closet," she answered, as he closed the window behind her. "And I was right."

"I'm sorry."

"Don't apologize to me. I wasn't the one you went all 'Hey, babe, don't tie me down' with."

"I meant it to be harsh," he said flatly. "We were getting to the point in the relationship where I was either going to have to score a touchdown or fake a fumble."

"That's the most awkward sports analogy I've ever heard."

He grinned. "You know what I mean."

"She was going to expect you to sleep with her."

He nodded.

She feigned an indifference she didn't feel. "Most undercover operatives would consider that a perk of the job."

"It's not what I want. I don't like using people as it is. Using her that way would be damned near criminal."

"Glad to hear it." She handed him the satellite phone tucked in her pocket. "I put it on mute, so you'll need to check to see if Brand called."

Scanlon's expression darkened. "I need to call him about your extraction anyway."

He was pretty damned determined to be rid of her, too. For the same reasons he was shaking off Dahlia McCoy?

While Scanlon dialed the phone, Isabel sat on the bed and opened the file folder, trying to ignore his call while she ran over the notes again.

Scanlon hung up. "Still no answer."

Isabel frowned. "Should we worry?"

"If he's in a high-level meeting at the Bureau, he can't drop everything to answer. But if we leave it much longer, there'll be no way to set up an extraction by tonight."

"So eager to be shed of me," she murmured.

He turned to look at her, his eyes dark with feeling. "I'm dreading it. But I want you safe."

Warmth spread in her chest and tears pricked her eyes. "We really do work better together than apart."

Sitting next to her, he nudged her with his shoulder, a gesture she'd come to consider a sign of affection. "Maybe that's one reason I'm trying to distance myself from Dahlia."

She nudged his shoulder back. "Can't handle more than one woman in your bed at a time?"

He turned to look at her, his expression more serious than she'd expected after her attempt to lighten the mood. "I don't *want* more than one woman in my bed."

Scanlon's gaze was all smoky-blue intensity, sending a shudder of need racing through Isabel's body, a fierce, primal longing to take him inside her, to claim him as hers just as surely as he'd brand her as his own.

The satellite phone trilled, rattling Isabel's nerves. She looked away, feeling edgy and breathless.

"I was beginning to wonder if I needed to send someone to track you down," Scanlon was saying into the phone. After a second, he added, "I think we need to reconsider that—it's getting too dangerous—"

Brand must have interrupted, for Scanlon went silent again, just listening. His thoughts were hard to read in his expression, which seemed to vacillate between alarm and an odd sort of reluctant pleasure. Finally, he spoke again: "I understand. Will do, sir." He shut off the phone and turned to look at Isabel. "He doesn't want to do the extraction before Addie's party tomorrow afternoon."

She was surprised, not so much that Brand had wanted her there with Scanlon but by how little Scanlon had put up a fight. He'd seemed so determined to get her out of Bolen Bluff tonight. Aloud, she just said, "Okay," and gave a brief nod.

"I'm sorry."

"I'm not," she said bluntly.

"I hope you don't have any reason to change your

mind about that," he responded, shoving the phone into his pocket and heading for the bedroom door. "But for now, I've got to go out to the drop site."

She followed him out of the room. "In broad daylight?"

"He doesn't think we should let this delivery sit out there too long. The risk of discovery is too great." Scanlon started to put the satellite phone into its box, then stopped, looking at her. He handed the phone to her. "Put it on mute again, but it'll vibrate slightly. Answer it if it rings."

She took the phone and walked with him into the front room. "What, exactly, are we in such a hurry to pick up from the barn?"

He grabbed his camouflage jacket from the arm of the futon sofa and shrugged it on. "A new way of interacting with the world outside," he answered with a grin.

"Which, translated to normal-people English, means?"

His grin broadened. "Daddy finally got us that computer we've always wanted."

SCANLON MADE THE TRIP to the drop site without incident, easily locating the plastic-wrapped devices the Huntsville FBI couriers had left hidden beneath the old corn bin. He tucked the bundle inside the camouflage backpack he'd borrowed back from Isabel and hiked back up the mountain to the cabin without spotting any signs of other humans in the woods.

She was waiting impatiently in the bedroom. "You want me to set it up for you?"

Flattering, he thought with a hint of amusement. "You have such faith in my abilities."

"You're not a computer expert."

"And you are?"

She made a face. "Do we really want to examine the history of our past encounters with high technology?"

"No," he admitted. He'd usually turned to her for help with any technological disasters he had encountered. "Brand said there'd be a note inside." He finished unwrapping the notebook computer from the padded plastic. Also inside the same packaging was a smartphone and a couple of simple connector cables. He set them aside and opened the notebook computer.

As promised, a single sheet of notepaper lay inside. Several lines of instructions scrawled across the page.

Written in German.

Isabel had taken German in college—which Brand would certainly know. A crude but probably effective form of cryptology, in these backwoods, at least. "This is for you."

"Hmm." She studied the page, her brow furrowed. "First, it says to set up a password." She looked up at him. In unison, they said, "Robert Frost."

He smiled—one of the first things they'd bonded

over as partners was their enjoyment of Frost's poetry.

"That works," he said, watching as she set up the password. "All one word, lowercase?"

"Yeah." She finished and picked up the note. "The next part tells us how to set up internet access with the cell phone, but I think I can handle that."

Scanlon moved out of the way and let her settle on the bed beside the computer. She powered up the laptop and connected the smartphone with a small cord. A few touches on the display panel later, a search engine popped onto the screen.

"The note also said to look for a file named 'Coopon' in the documents folder." She slanted a look at Scanlon. "That's his choice of a portmanteau for us? Really?"

She found the file. It contained a web address, a date and a time. "Today at 3:00 p.m." Isabel looked at the clock. "Ten minutes from now. Brand does love cutting it close."

"Where does the web address go?"

She typed the address into a browser window and reached a web chat portal. A dialogue box asked for a user name.

"Coopon?" Scanlon suggested.

"If it is, I'll kill him." She typed it in. An error message came up.

"Try the computer user name you used at the FBI." That name had been straightforward—last name, first initial.

She typed those letters in and clicked the button. The chat window came up and she was in.

So were five other chatters. Their screen names were just two letters each, each one ending in the letter C.

"Your family?"

"Early as always." Isabel nodded, her eyes suspiciously shiny. "JC is Jesse, RC is Rick—"

"And Megan, Wade and Shannon," he finished with a smile. He'd been an only child himself, missing out on being part of a family full of brothers and sisters. He'd never told Isabel, but he'd always enjoyed hearing about her family, even when she was exasperated with them.

Maybe especially when she was exasperated with them.

He sat back and enjoyed the family reunion, his gaze transfixed by the joy in Isabel's face as she caught up with her brothers and sisters. Apparently her father was there, too, though he didn't have a screen name in the chat room. Her eldest brother, Jesse, explained his dad was sitting with him at the Cooper Security office, watching everything.

By the time all the greetings were finished, Isabel was fighting tears. Scanlon rubbed her back, pleased when she leaned against him, rubbing her cheek against his shoulder.

Soon, however, the conversation went to the trouble at hand. When her brother Rick asked what was really going on with her and Scanlon, she turned her gaze to Scanlon as if asking permission to tell the truth.

He shook his head. "I know you trust them, and I trust you. But I can't let this get out."

The look she gave him was full of disappointment mingling with understanding. She turned back to the computer and typed in a quick message, telling them she couldn't explain anything at the moment.

"See if your brother Rick can tell me who the guy who calls himself Jeff Munroe might really be," Scanlon suggested. He fed her the description in as much detail as he could remember.

She typed in the details, keys rattling as her practiced fingers flew across the keyboard. Within seconds, Rick came back with a name. "Toby Lavelle. Hot-headed Cajun from Houma, Louisiana. I've heard rumors about stuff he did while he was in the SSU that would curl your hair."

Scanlon wasn't surprised by the revelation. He'd had a feeling that "Jeff Munroe" was very bad news.

As he was about to tell Isabel to ask him about the mysterious Kurasawa, she preempted him by typing, "Ever heard of anyone named Kurasawa? Someone a rogue SSU agent might want to meet with?" He couldn't hold back a smile.

It was her brother Jesse who answered her question this time. "The only Kurasawa I can think of who'd fit the bill is Carlos Kurasawa, a Peruvian gunrunner."

Isabel shot a quick, worried look at Scanlon. "Gunrunner?" she murmured.

"I wouldn't be surprised," he answered.

"Why are you asking about Kurasawa?" Jesse asked in the chat window.

"We're not sure," Isabel answered. Aloud, she added, "Could the Swains be branching out into gunrunning?"

"I've thought for a while that they're interested in doing more than cooking crank and growing weed," Scanlon admitted.

"You're not going to tell us anything else, are you?" That was Megan, and even Scanlon, who'd never met her, could read the exasperation through the computer screen.

"I can't," Isabel answered. "Let's talk about something else—how's Amanda, Rick? You enjoying married life?"

While Rick answered his sister in a series of quick blurbs to the affirmative, Scanlon got up from the bed and crossed to the window, gazing out at the waning day. Soon night would fall, cocooning him and Isabel in darkness yet again. He didn't want to waste a single minute of time with her, now that her day of departure was set. She'd leave tomorrow night, after he filled in at the feed store.

She'd walk out of his life again, with no guarantee they'd ever see each other again.

He turned back to the bed. "I'm going to go see if I can whip something up for dinner," he murmured, bending low to speak in her ear. "You don't need to stay online too much longer—wrap it up in fifteen minutes."

She gave him a grateful smile and turned back to her screen to continue chatting with her family. He watched her a moment longer, warmth running through him at the sight of her obvious happiness. As much as he didn't want to see her go, he could tell how much she missed her family.

She'd been away from them a long time while working for the FBI. Maybe being back with them for the last few months had reminded her just how much she enjoyed having family around.

As he searched his cabinets for something to prepare for dinner, he thought about his own family. His mother and stepfather were still alive, still together. Knowing his mother had George Scanlon to comfort her was the only thing that had allowed him to fake his own death. He was glad Isabel had been able to turn to her own family, as well.

He was the one who would be well and truly alone once she left him behind tomorrow evening.

He was still brooding over that thought when Isabel came into the kitchen fifteen minutes later on the dot. She was still smiling, her eyes bright and her cheeks pink with happiness. "I may have to officially forgive SAC Brand for lying to me about you."

He made a face. "Wow, you're easy."

"I didn't realize how much I missed them. We've

really reconnected over the last few months—all of us. We were all scattered for so long, and now we're all back home, working together—" She laughed, as if she realized she was gushing. "I'm just happy to have my family back."

He tried not to think about what his life would be like when she was gone again. Once she was back home, back among the people she clearly loved, maybe she'd begin to see that staying with him, putting her life on the line for him, would have been a terrible idea.

Maybe she wouldn't think much about him at all, once she was back home where she clearly belonged. He would be a memory, more pleasant now that she knew he hadn't died a horrible death in her place—

Stop, he scolded himself. *Stop feeling sorry for yourself. Just be glad she's going to be happy and safe.*

And he *was* glad. Knowing she'd be home, where her family would protect and support her, had to be enough for him.

"So, what're you fixing for dinner?" she asked, her drawl broader than usual and absolutely charming.

"Trying to decide," he admitted, opening the freezer. He'd bought a half chicken when he'd bought the salmon, but that seemed too big a project to tackle when his stomach was growling so loudly.

He'd also bought some hamburger meat, hoping to make a pot of chili, but it would take forever to thaw.

"Really should have started thinking about dinner about an hour ago," she murmured, a smile in her voice. She closed the freezer door and opened the refrigerator. "We have cherries, pears, grapes and mayo—I can make a fruit salad out of those. Sound good?"

He nodded. "It does."

"We need some protein—eggs. You bought eggs, you genius! We'll do omelets and fruit salad. And if you bought any bread, slap a little butter on it and some of that parmesan cheese I saw in the cabinet, and we'll have cheesy toast, too."

An omelet was one meal he could handle, so he went about whipping it up, adding chopped onion and red peppers to the mix to give it a little more zing. Isabel tackled the parmesan toast and the fruit salad, and within fifteen minutes they had a nice meal laid out on the rickety card table. He even broke out the better brand of paper plates, making her smile.

"I don't have any hooch around here," he admitted, "but I bought a nice bottle of orange juice. Chateau Sunshine State." He showed her the bottle.

She made a show of checking the expiration date stamped on the bottle label. "Ah, a very good month!"

He grinned at her. "You're an easy date, Isabel Cooper."

She arched an eyebrow at him. "Did you just call me easy?"

He shook his head, handing her a fork and sitting in the chair across from her. "You're anything but easy."

She smiled at him. "And don't you forget it."

He wouldn't, he knew. He wouldn't forget anything about her, not if he lived a hundred years. She was permanently imprinted on him, an indelible part of his life that time and distance would never erase.

He just wasn't sure how he was going to live without her after having her back in his life again for this brief, sweet moment of time.

Chapter Twelve

Isabel could see the uncertainty in Scanlon's eyes when she asked him for a deck of cards. "I thought Solitaire was your game," he said, as he dug a dog-eared pack from one of the kitchen drawers.

She gave the pack a skeptical look. "Judging by the state of these cards, it looks like Solitaire is *your* game."

"Hah." He pushed the deck toward her. "What's your poison? Five-card stud? Blackjack? Texas Hold 'Em?"

"Do you even know what those games are?"

"Not really," he admitted. He watched her hands as she shuffled the cards. "Why do I get the strange feeling I'm about to be fleeced?"

"This game is easy. Very straightforward. My cousins Jake and Gabe invented it, and I can't believe I haven't introduced you to it before now." She tried to hold back a grin, rather enjoying his look of wary interest. It was a rare thing indeed to be able to introduce Ben Scanlon to something he wasn't familiar with. He had an insane amount of both common and arcane knowledge stored up inside that brilliant mind of his.

"Why do you look so damned gleeful?" he asked suspiciously.

"Here's how you play," she continued, ignoring his question. "Each player gets half the deck. You lay out your cards at the same time, one at a time. The person with the high card gets to ask the person with the low card any question she wants."

"Or he wants?"

"Of course," she said reluctantly. Not that she thought Scanlon could ask her anything much that he didn't already know about her. She'd been a lot more open with him than she suspected he'd been with her.

Which was why she'd thought about playing a game of Popsmack in the first place.

"Popsmack?" he questioned when she told him the name of the game. "What kind of stupid name for a game is that?"

"I think it grew organically out of the resulting fisticuffs between my cousins when they played the game," she explained, dealing out the deck evenly between them.

"Are these the cousins who fish?"

She chuckled. "They are indeed. Gabe and Jake—they're twins. They actually fished the tournament tour a couple of years. Did pretty well—both of them bought houses outright with their winnings, so I guess they know what they're doing."

"About fishing, at least," he conceded. "Not sure about card games."

"Oh, quit whining." She finished dealing the cards and put her hand on the top card. "You go first."

"I thought we laid them out at the same time."

"Okay fine. One, two, three, deal."

They each laid a card on the table. Isabel's was a seven of spades. Scanlon's was a nine of hearts.

"There. You win," she said. "Not so bad, is it?"

His smile was wicked. "Not for me, anyway."

She felt a little flutter of apprehension as he made a show of thinking up a question. "You know, it's perfectly fine to ask a person her favorite color or something like that."

"Your favorite color is turquoise blue. Every bloody knickknack you ever put on your desk was that color." He shook his head. "I'm thinking of something a little more, you know…personal."

She tried not to react, since he clearly wanted her to. "Okay, shoot."

"What was your most memorable date in high school?"

"Thank you for assuming I dated in high school," she said with a soft laugh. "I did, but not until my senior year—orthodontics took a toll on my sex appeal up to that point." She gave the question some serious thought. "You did say memorable, right?"

He nodded, looking genuinely interested in her answer.

"It was homecoming of my senior year. The braces had been off since the previous summer, and guys were actually starting to see me as something other than a walking metal grin." It had been a heady time, those days, when she'd actually started believing her father's assurances that she was a pretty girl. "Trent Jameson—football player, very popular, kind of hot in that jock sort of way—asked me out for homecoming and actually meant it. Not as a joke or anything."

"Good grief, those first three years of high school must have been a doozy," Scanlon murmured.

"So the day before homecoming Trent and some of his friends had gone hiking up Gossamer Mountain. It was October, but still kind of warm, and they ended up taking off their jackets and hiking in short sleeves. Through really thick woods." She winced, remembering how Trent had looked the day of the homecoming dance.

"Let me guess—leaves of three, let them be— only he didn't?"

"Exactly. Trent was covered with poison ivy rash, his poor face was swollen up until he was unrecognizable. There I was, my first real date, with one of the coolest guys in school, and he looked like something out of a Japanese monster movie."

Scanlon laughed. "Poor Trent."

"Poor me! It took the rest of the year to live down my instant reputation as a jinx date." She laughed, now that she was long past the horror. "College was better." She reached for the next card on the deck and laid down a ten of spades.

Scanlon dealt a six of diamonds. "Uh oh."

What to ask? She wondered whether she should ease him in or go straight for the things she really wanted to know.

"Be gentle," he pleaded softly.

"You're a big guy. You can take it." She took a deep breath and plunged in. "Why did you become an FBI agent?"

The question seemed to catch him completely by surprise. "I—I don't know, really. I guess the usual thing—I wanted to help people. I thought the FBI would be a good place to do that, so I added an accounting degree to my English degree because I knew the FBI looked for accountants."

It was a perfectly reasonable answer, she had to admit. But she didn't believe a bit of it.

He had another reason for joining the FBI. She'd known that about him for a long time, though he never showed any inclination to share his motivations with her.

She was beginning to wonder if he ever would.

TOLLIVER FEED AND SEED had closed at five that evening, but Opal Swain knew her sister would still be in the back, counting the day's receipts. The feed store itself would have been perpetually in the red, of course, if it had depended only on sales, but the store actually existed to launder the money earned from methamphetamine and marijuana sales, so it would never go under. Not as long as there were fools who wanted to alter their consciousnesses.

Opal herself had never sampled the family wares. She didn't even drink, knowing full well that her most marketable asset was her mind.

She had never been pretty, like Addie and their sister, Melinda, had been when they were younger. But she'd been smart. Smart enough to marry Earl Butler and support his hardworking ways. Smart enough to get J.T. out of Bolen Bluff when it looked like he was aiming to be as shiftless as the rest of his cousins, whose only goals in life seemed to be growing weed and cooking meth until the next generation took over the business.

Smart enough to realize when it was time to come home and claim her rightful place at the head of the Swain household.

The front door was locked, but Opal had a key. The business had belonged to their father long before Addie and her lazy husband took over the shop twenty years ago. He'd left it to all of them equally; Addie had been the only one who'd wanted to run it. It had given her husband, Carl, something to do to keep out of trouble and other women's britches, and Addie had enjoyed the position it had put her in—right in the throbbing heart of the family business.

Addie looked up in surprise when Opal entered

her office without knocking. "Damn it, Opal, you scared the hell out of me. You can't knock?"

"Don't need to knock. The place belongs to me, too."

Addie's lips flattened to a thin line. The lively beauty she'd possessed as a girl was long gone now, stolen by time and a harsh and ugly life. Of the two of them, Opal was the more attractive now, though neither of them would turn heads anymore.

"There somethin' you want?" Addie asked.

"I want more to do with the business. I'm good with books. You never had much of a head for numbers."

"I do all right."

"You get by. The business could be doing more."

"Do a whole lot more, and people will start takin' notice of what we're doing here. Nobody wants that."

"They already notice, Addie. We're always livin' on borrowed time. Always."

"And you want to stir things up and bring that time crashin' down on us even faster?" Addie asked bluntly.

"Time is already crashin' down on us. We got strong young wolves snappin' at our heels."

"You think Leamon and the boys are gonna give us trouble? They don't know how to find their backsides with their own two hands," Addie scoffed.

"It's not those boys I'm worried about." Opal didn't elaborate. If Addie didn't see the danger lurking around her, Opal felt no particular obligation to point it out. Sometimes the herd needed culling, and Opal didn't mind if someone else did it for her.

"Did you come by here for a particular reason, or did you just want to lord it over me about what a bad job you think I'm doin'?" Addie returned to adding up the day's haul in her tiny, crooked handwriting. None of the family trusted computers, of course—the paper trail was so much harder to control. But someone should have replaced Addie in the bookkeeping job long ago. Her sister had never been good at math, and there was no telling how much family money was being siphoned away at the ground level because Addie couldn't keep track.

"I was serious about the books."

Addie looked up at her, exasperation etched in every line on her aging face. "If I start thinkin' I need your help, I'll be sure to give you a call."

Opal had every right to take a stand here, to demand her full share of the business. But she also knew that a confrontation with her sister at this point, when Addie held the position of strength in the family, would be a fool's game.

Change was coming, and Addie wouldn't be able to weather the storm. She wasn't smart enough or nimble enough.

Opal could bide her time. Wait for the opening she needed. It would come, sooner than later.

She changed the subject. "Davy McCoy said

you'd asked Mark Shipley to watch the store tomorrow durin' the barbecue."

"I did."

"What do you know about him?"

"He gets along good with the boys. Dahlia McCoy's got the shivers for him. God knows the boy needs money, and he's willin' to do just about anything the boys ask of him."

"Have they asked for somethin' special from him?"

Addie shot her a sly look. "Not yet."

So Addie had invited Shipley to work at the feed store as a test of some sort. What was her sister up to? "How do you know he's not a fed undercover?"

"The boys have been keeping an eye on him. Checkin' his place when he's out. They took him down to see some people—" Addie hushed up quickly. Opal swallowed a smile—her sister could never keep a secret, even when she tried.

Of course, Opal knew all about the mercenaries. She even knew what they were up to here in Halloran County.

There wasn't much that went on around here these days that she hadn't made her business.

Maybe she should add Mark Shipley to that list.

SCANLON WAS FEELING ENTIRELY too relaxed and content. He knew it was a dangerous combination, especially with the constant threat of discovery haunting his every step.

But it felt so good—so right—having Isabel with him again. Setting aside the relentless simmer of attraction that kept his heart pounding and his skin prickling, he'd missed her sharp humor and quick mind. She was his anchor, in the best sense of the word, and he'd felt absolutely lost without her.

It was going to be hell letting go of her again.

"We need to take this party into the bedroom," he said. The sloe-eyed glance she slanted his way made his gut tighten into a knot. "It's not really safe up here," he added, his voice oddly hoarse.

Her lips curved but she dutifully gathered up the remains of their card game and tucked the deck into the pocket of her jeans. She nodded toward the radio sitting on the counter near the stove. "Can we take the radio?"

"Sure." She'd turned the radio to a classic rock station out of Georgia earlier, and the evening DJ was on a serious Southern rock kick—a little Skynyrd, a little Charlie Daniels, some Allman Brothers. He didn't mind a little Southern-fried head-banging, either.

By the time they reached the bedroom and plugged the radio in, the opening beats of .38 Special's "Second Chance" was pouring through the speakers, tinny but infectious.

Isabel's eyes lit up. "I love this song!" She started to dance, her lithe limbs moving with surprising grace as she caught the beat. "Come on, Scanlon, you can't tell me this doesn't make you want to tap your toe."

He managed a smile, completely entranced by the sinuous play of her long limbs as she danced toward him across the bedroom floor. When she grabbed his hand and tugged him closer, he gave up trying to resist and let her draw him into the dance.

He wrapped one arm around her slim waist and pulled her to him, swaying against her as he listened to the lyrics, a plaintive plea for a second chance at love and forgiveness.

"Too much light in here, don't you think?" She danced away from him and flicked on the small lamp by the bed, then shimmied over to the wall to turn off the overhead light. Shadows descended on the room, cocooning them in oddly comforting darkness. She slipped back into his arms, laying her head in the curve of his neck.

"Here we are again," she whispered a few minutes later, her breath warm against his throat. "Right where we always seem to end up. One foot in forever and the other in never."

The pain in her voice made his chest hurt. "I know."

"I don't want to leave here with any regrets," she said.

He sighed, the ache settling somewhere in the vicinity of his heart. "I know." He let her go.

She licked her lips, reached into her pocket and

pulled out the dog-eared deck of cards. She plucked two off the top, facedown. "Pick one."

He eyed her warily. "What are you doing?"

"Pick a card. One last round of Popsmack."

He pulled a card from her hand and looked at it. Four of clubs. That didn't bode well. He looked up at her. She was studying the card in her hand, her look reflective.

"What do you have?" he asked.

She flipped the card over and showed him the two of diamonds. "You win."

He held her gaze, his heart in his throat. He had a sneaking suspicion that she'd cheated to get the low card, but he couldn't stop himself from asking the question burning in his brain. "What do you want to happen now, Isabel? The truth."

She took the card from his hand and stacked it on top of the deck, setting it on the dresser. She closed the distance between them, rising to her tiptoes to whisper in his ear.

Her blunt, honest answer sent a shiver down his spine.

"Are you sure?" he asked.

She gazed at him with shining eyes. "If we step away this time, we may never get another chance to get it right."

He threaded his fingers through her curls, pulling her closer again. "Are you sure this is right?"

"No," she admitted, rising to her toes again. Her lips rasped across his beard stubble. "But it's worth the risk, don't you think?" She dropped a kiss along the tendon at the side of his throat, making him groan as heat exploded low in his belly.

He wanted her. More than he wanted his next breath. So much that he couldn't stop his hands from shaking as he cradled her face and bent his head to kiss her.

She tasted as sweet as pears, as tart as cherries. As dark as midnight and just as seductive. He couldn't have resisted the slow, determined exploration of her hands on his body, utterly disarmed by her touch.

She stepped back, evoking a low growl of frustration from his throat, but she retreated only long enough to shrug out of her soft cotton T-shirt. The lavender lace of her bra was a delightful surprise, a silken reminder of the woman who lay hidden beneath the facade of the capable, pulled-together FBI agent he'd worked with every day for almost seven years.

"You need me to undress you, too?" she asked with a wicked smile, shimmying out of her jeans to reveal a pair of turquoise-blue bikini briefs.

He couldn't stop a chuckle at the mismatched underwear. Somehow, the fashion failure only made her that much sexier. He shed his own shirt at record speed and cursed his choice of button-fly jeans that morning when he was getting dressed. He fumbled at the buttons until she crossed to him and made quick work of them, helping him yank the jeans down over his hips. He stepped out of them, kicked them out of the way and reached for her.

She was silky soft and fiery hot, vibrating with life and intensity, going to his head like hard liquor until he was dizzy and hot. He followed her lead back to his bed, falling on top of her when she pulled him down with her.

Her thighs parted and he positioned himself between them, not at all surprised by how perfectly their bodies fit together. He stayed utterly still a moment, just enjoying the sensations of her skin on his, the tremors moving up and down his spine in rhythm with his hammering heart.

She moved her hands slowly up his sides, fingertips tracing lazy circles over his skin. She smiled up at him, anticipation sparkling in her eyes. "I already like this better than our usual modus operandi."

"Now you're just trying to make me hot."

"Is it working?" Her fingers danced along the ridge of his spine, scattering shivers along the trail she blazed.

He rocked his hips against hers. "What do you think?"

"I think we're entirely overdressed."

He slid his hands under her, finding the hooks of her bra. He tugged them loose and plucked the lacy fabric out of the way, letting it drop to the floor.

He pressed his mouth to the ripe curve of her left breast and kissed his way from one side to the other.

Her low moan of pleasure was like gasoline on the fire in his belly.

He looked up to find Isabel gazing at him with desire-drunk eyes, her expression serious. "How am I going to say goodbye to you?" she whispered.

He lowered his mouth slowly to hers, kissing her with all the urgency that burned in the center of his aching chest. Her arms wrapped around his neck, pulling him closer until he felt her breasts flattened against his chest.

They made love with quiet intensity, each touch, each whisper, each groan of pleasure and passion a reminder of how fleeting the time remaining between them really was.

He felt her come apart in his arms, her low growl of release like air to a drowning man. He let go, unraveled, twined himself around her until he wasn't sure he existed anymore. He was part of her. She was part of him.

And tomorrow, he thought, pain ripping through his chest, he would have to find a way to let her go.

Chapter Thirteen

A static-edged Eagles ballad drifted through the room, the melancholy tone settling in the center of Isabel's chest. Beneath her cheek, Scanlon's heart had finally slowed to a steady cadence, slipping into rhythm with her own.

His hand played lightly in her hair, wrapping her curls around his fingers. "So that's what we were missing."

She leaned her head back to look up at him in the dim, golden light. Though she was finally used to his scruffier appearance, a sense of uncertainty struck a hammer blow to her confidence. In so many ways, he was no longer the man she thought she knew almost as well as she knew herself.

Maybe he never had been.

"Are you sorry?" she asked, hating herself for the display of insecurity but unable to remain silent.

He looked at her as if she'd lost her mind. "No."

"I thought it would somehow make things easier if we just stopped trying to fight it—"

"I don't think it's supposed to be easy," he murmured, sliding his finger along the chain of the locket around her neck. He gave it a light tug. "It's only easy if it doesn't really matter. If there aren't consequences."

"I'm still going to be leaving tomorrow. You're still going to be staying." The bald statement of reality escaped her throat in a sigh.

"That's right." His mouth tightened a little. "But I can't be sorry about having this memory to keep me company when you're gone."

"You're such a girl, Scanlon." Tears burned her eyes, tempering her teasing smile.

He turned his blistering gaze to her, sending a jolt of pure need rattling through her. "You looking to provoke me into proving otherwise?"

She kissed his collarbone. "I take it back. You're all man." And then some.

"If I didn't have to go work at the feed store tomorrow, we could spend the rest of our time together in bed," he murmured, regret darkening his voice.

"Instead, you should get a good night's sleep so you'll be on top of your game." She started to roll away from him, but he tugged her closer.

"No. I'll sleep better if you're here." He spooned her close, his chin resting against the top of her head. His fingers found the locket around her neck and started playing with it again. Finally, his fingers went still.

She fell silent for a while, fighting against a fierce

tide of dread rising in her chest until she felt as if she were drowning. She had experienced the same sensation twice before. Once the day Adam Brand told her that Scanlon had died in the explosion. And, even earlier, the day her father told her that her mother had left and was going to live somewhere else now.

The flood of memories from her childhood battered her heart until she couldn't stay quiet. "Are you asleep?"

"No," he answered, his breath warm on her cheek.

"Did I ever tell you about what it was like for me when my mother went away?"

He was silent a moment. "You told me she left when you were young and that you don't see that much of her anymore."

She nodded. "All true. But what I never told you was how many weeks I spent haunting our front door, absolutely positive that Mama would come walking through it again and tell us that it was just a silly joke she'd been playing on us all."

"Oh, baby." Scanlon brushed his lips across her temple.

"Mamas aren't supposed to go away forever." Blinking back tears, she added, "Not on purpose."

"How often do you see her now?"

"Once or twice a year, if she's in the area. I actually ran into her once, in D.C. She was in town for a symposium on surgical advances—she's a surgical nurse. Travels the world teaching other nurses."

"Oh. Was that when we were working that child abduction case and you nearly bit my head off when I suggested listening to one of the psychics who'd crawled out of the woodworks?"

She rolled over to look at him, chuckling. "I always snap at you when you suggest stupid things like that."

"But that time, I think you broke the skin." His lips curved. "I could tell something was eating at you—was that it? Seeing your mom?"

"At the time, I just thought I reacted that way because you were suggesting something crazy and completely unscientific, but, yeah. Probably."

"It didn't go well?"

"It went fine. She was pleased to see me." Her chest tightened. "As if I were some college roommate she hadn't seen in a while. Not her daughter."

"I'm sorry. That must have hurt."

"I'm okay. So much luckier than most. My dad's brothers have wonderful wives who took up the slack. Aunt Beth and Aunt Sandy took turns making sure we had a mother figure around all the time. Aunt Beth was a nurse, and she taught us all we know about first aid. Uncle Mike and Dad took us all out fishing on Gossamer Lake. And Aunt Sandy is an artist—she tried to teach us all about art and the finer things." She made a face. "It didn't really take with me."

"No, you're not really the artsy sort," he agreed. "If I recall correctly, the extent of your art appre-

ciation is your inexplicable fascination with Wedg-
wood jasperware."

"It looks like a frosted blue cake," she defended.
"I like blue. And cake."

He hugged her closer, his laughter warm against
her cheek. "How the hell am I going to let you leave
me tomorrow?"

"Maybe I could dye my hair and cut it off. Wear
colored contacts—they might not even be able to
recognize me. I could come back as your cousin
with the abusive husband—"

He groaned. "As tempting as that idea is, it's entirely too dangerous. I'm already skating the edge
here. They don't trust me yet, and one wrong move
could get us both killed before Brand or the FBI
could do a damned thing about it."

She knew he was right, no matter how much she
longed to believe there was a way she could stay
here with him. "I want to stay involved in the case,
somehow."

"You're not even an FBI agent anymore—"

"Brand owes me. And I can help. He can treat me
like a consultant. I wouldn't even charge him for my
time."

"This case could go for years. You know that."

"I don't care—"

"I do," he said bluntly, cradling her face to make
her look up at him. "I don't want you to spend the
prime of your life worrying about me. You need to
have your own life."

She flinched a little at the hard determination in his smoky blue eyes. "You want me to walk away? Not look back?"

She saw the answer in his expression, the pain her words evoked. But his words were simple. "Yes. That's what I want."

Isabel pulled away from him, turning to look at the wall. She didn't know whether to fume or ache. "I don't believe you."

"This case isn't the only thing standing between us. We went seven years together without acting on our desires."

"Everything was complicated. Our jobs—"

"It's not against the rules to sleep with your co-worker. We both know married FBI agents who work together."

She couldn't argue. "I didn't want to upset the balance."

"And you don't really believe in love."

She turned to look at him. "Oh, I believe in love. I just don't believe it lasts forever. Not for most people."

"And you'd rather have nothing at all than something that can be taken away from you in a heart-beat."

She couldn't argue with that observation, either.

He plucked at her locket, his gaze lowered. "I can't commit myself to anything but the work I'm doing. I'm in it for the long haul. I don't have room for anything else."

"Does it have to be for the FBI? Couldn't you work for someone else?"

He looked up. "Work for your brother, you mean?"

"You're the kind of person he hires. Hard-working, smart, resourceful, FBI trained—"

"I'm not leaving the FBI, Cooper."

Not for me, you mean. Rolling over, she gazed up at the shadows cast by the bedside lamp on the ceiling.

"Don't do this," he pleaded softly. "Don't overanalyze things. I don't regret being with you, even if it never happens again. I'm glad you're here with me right now. I'm grateful I got to see you one more time before we have to part again."

"And I'm glad you're alive," she whispered, slanting her gaze in his direction. Hot tears trickled from her eyes and down her cheeks to wet the pillow.

He slid his arm around her, pulling her to him. Laying her head on his chest, she listened to the now-familiar percussion of his heartbeat against her ear. He kissed her temple and whispered in her ear, "Remember what you told me you wanted? When I won that last game of Smackpop?"

She chuckled. "Popsmack. And yeah. I remember."

"I want the same thing you did."

She arched an eyebrow. "Now? You're really ready for that, sport?"

He nibbled lightly at the side of her neck, one hand sliding down to cup the curve of her breast.

"Oh, I'm ready." He shifted toward her, revealing just how ready he was.

Curling her fingers in his hair to draw him closer, she kissed him, tasting his dark, rich flavor. She wanted to memorize it, memorize him. The sound of his voice, the rasp of his hands on her skin. The naked desire in his eyes as he gazed at her. Burned for her.

He snaked his arms around her waist and rolled her on top of him, his hands trembling on her hips, a testament to just how much he wanted her—and how willing he was to let her take control. "Your turn," he growled.

Her heart stuttered into higher gear.

He had been quiet, intense the first time they made love, but even as he let her take the lead this time, he talked to her, telling her what he liked. What she was doing to him. What he wanted for her.

By the time she collapsed in his arms, shaking and beyond spent, all he whispered was her name, over and over, as if trying to imprint it on his brain.

A thought hit her as she listened to his soft recitation, an idea so melancholy it made her heart hurt.

Maybe he was memorizing her, too.

THE NIGHT AIR WAS COLD, his breath visible in the pale moonlight. He wasn't supposed to be outside—Daddy had told him to go find Mama and stay inside. But he wasn't a baby anymore, and he could tell Daddy was worried.

He might need backup.

His jacket seemed thin and useless, the February chill seeping through the thin cotton weave. Daffodils lining the driveway seemed to shiver in the westerly breeze, as if deeply regretting their decision to make an early appearance.

He stumbled on a crack in the concrete, pitching forward before catching himself. But the stumble had foiled his attempt at stealth, and Daddy turned around at the sound.

"Benny, I told you to find your Mama and stay inside."

"You can't go out without backup."

The exasperated love in his father's eyes eclipsed the anxious expression for a brief moment. "I appreciate that, chief, but you don't have your badge yet—"

The hum of a vehicle engine drifted toward them on the breeze. His father broke off and turned his attention toward the sound.

There was a vehicle coming up the road.

Old Mentone Highway saw a moderate amount of traffic during the daylight hours, but after dark, the number of vehicles that passed down the winding mountain road greatly decreased.

"Get back inside, Benny," his father ordered. He cocked the rifle he carried.

But Ben couldn't move. He froze in place, watching his father set himself like one of those rangy Western heroes Ben and his dad liked to watch on television—Marshal Dillon, or the Rifleman, maybe.

The sound of the truck grew louder, muffler rattling. The engine gunned and suddenly there it was—

Ben tried to see the truck more clearly, but it was a blur. A big black blur.

He tried to see the faces behind the windshield, but moonlight cast a glare.

The truck window lowered. A face appeared in the window.

But it was blank and featureless. A pale spot in the middle of a void.

The crack of a gunshot split the air.

His father fell. Down, down, down. The ground seemed to shake beneath Ben's feet as his father hit the driveway, already spilling blood onto the concrete.

He looked at the truck again. Tried to memorize everything.

But there was nothing to see. It had disappeared into the ether. Everything around him had faded into gray nothingness. No house. No trees. No daffodils shivering in the cold.

Just his father's body, crumpled and bloodstained, and the rapid-fire percussion of his own racing heart.

Scanlon woke with a start, sitting upright. He was in his bedroom in the cabin. The air was warm, heated by the gas unit just outside in the hallway. He was naked.

And Isabel Cooper sat curled up in a chair near the window, dressed in his blue plaid shirt and a pair of his white cotton socks. She looked up from the file she was reading and smiled at him, setting his whole body ablaze with the memory of their night together.

"Good morning," she said.

"What are you doing way over there?"

"Reading your files."

"Workaholic," he grumbled. "Come back over here."

She got up and walked over to the bed, her bare legs stretching for miles beneath the hem of his shirt. He felt himself growing harder by the second. "I found something odd."

"You're not seriously going to try to talk business, are you?" he asked, reaching his hand out to her.

She ignored his hand and sat on the edge of the bed, facing him. "This is important."

He pushed aside the quilt covering his lap. "So's this."

She arched an eyebrow at him. "Can I at least tell you what I found?"

He grimaced. "Okay, fine. What did you find?"

"This." She showed him one of the reports stored in the file, a missing persons report for someone named Trey Pritchard.

Scanlon searched his memory until he placed

the name. "Right. Pritchard was a guy who'd approached the DEA about twelve years ago. Claimed to have some inside information about the Swain family. But he never showed for the meeting, according to the DEA agent he'd contacted. The agent tracked down his family, learned Pritchard hadn't been in touch with them for weeks, and so they filed a missing persons report."

"Trey Pritchard was the brother of my friend Annie," Isabel said. She picked up the locket hanging around her neck. "*This* Annie."

Scanlon's brow rose in surprise. "Small world."

"Annie was killed in a bombing at their home. The same home Trey shared with her and their parents—"

Scanlon realized where she was going. "You think the bomb could have been meant for Trey?"

"If he was trying to narc on the Swains, yeah." She reached back to unfasten the catch of the necklace chain.

"I wonder why that information wasn't included in the missing persons report."

"There's a mention that he'd lost his sister to murder a couple of months earlier. Doesn't specify how she was killed."

His earlier ardor cooled by Isabel's troubling discovery, Scanlon rolled off the bed and started getting dressed. When he was clad in jeans and another plaid shirt, he turned around and saw that Isabel had pulled on a pair of slim-fitting yoga pants.

She still wore his shirt, looking better in it than he could have ever hoped to. She sat cross-legged in the middle of the messy bed, atop the quilt, and studied the locket she'd unfastened from around her neck.

"Trey gave me this locket almost a month after Annie's death," she said, as he crossed to where she sat. "I wondered at the time why he was the one who gave it to me and not Annie's mom."

He held out his hand for the locket, and she handed it over. He pried at the latch that should have opened the locket to reveal whatever lay inside. But it didn't budge.

He took a closer look. "I think this locket has been soldered together."

She took it from him and peered more closely at it. "You're right. I can see the little drops of solder."

"It should be easy to pry open." He had a multi-purpose utility knife in his belt pack. He dug it from the drawer where he kept it stored and pulled out the knife.

"Why would he give it to me?"

"Maybe because he knew where he could find you, and he didn't figure anyone from the Swain family would know to look for you." He took the locket back from her, studying the way it was soldered together. There were actually two drops of solder, carefully placed so that the simple pressure of tugging at the latch wouldn't exert enough force to break through the solder.

He slid the narrow blade of the utility knife into

the tiny seam between the locket wings and gave it a twist. One piece of solder cracked open. A second twist took care of the other. The locket sprang open.

Isabel scooted closer to see what he'd uncovered. Her eyebrows arching, she looked up at Scanlon, confusion in her dark eyes. "What the hell?"

Scanlon dragged his gaze away from Isabel's puzzled expression and again looked down at the opened locket. There were no photos framed in either wing of the locket, as he might have expected.

Instead, nestled in the otherwise empty frame on the right wing lay a small gold key.

Chapter Fourteen

Isabel picked up the key. It was barely small enough to fit in the locket. Turning it over, she saw a strip of tape adhered to the key head, with a number in fading blue ink—112.

"A locker key?" Scanlon guessed. "Could be the number."

"But what kind of locker?"

"How well did you know Trey Pritchard?"

"Not well. He was older than Annie. Didn't get along with the new stepfather. Drug use kept him from holding on to a job, and Mr. Lewis rode him pretty hard about it. The family was having enough trouble dealing with racist freaks as it was—they didn't need Trey bringing problems home to add to the nightmare."

"Nobody thought his drug connections might have been behind the attack on the family home?"

Isabel shook her head. "Trey hadn't lived there for months, and the family had been dealing with harassment because Mr. Lewis was black." She tamped down the anger that rose in her gut when she remembered what her friend had gone through in the months before her death. "Everyone thought it was the Klan or some other white supremacist group."

"Did they look for the bomb signature, at least?"

"I don't know. All I thought about at the time was how empty my life would be without my friend," Isabel admitted. "I can find out—I have cousins in the Sheriff's Department. If the evidence still exists, I should be able to find it there."

"What do you think the key unlocks?"

"There are bus stations in Maybridge and Gossamer Ridge, train and bus stations a county over in Borland—also a regional airport there, but I don't know if they offer locker storage." Isabel looked down at the key. "I can check when I get home."

As soon as the words slipped from her mouth, a sharp pain settled in the center of her solar plexus. Within twelve hours, she would be headed back to Gossamer Ridge. Scanlon would have to remain dead to her, as far as anyone outside her family knew.

There was no guarantee she'd ever see him again.

Scanlon ran his fingers down the curve of her jaw. "It's going to be okay, Cooper. I promise."

She shook her head. "Don't make promises you can't keep."

He dropped his hand away. "What do you think you'll find in the locker if you can locate it? Any idea?"

"I don't know. But he gave the locket to me a little while after Annie died. He said she'd want me to have it."

"Could the key belong to Annie?"

"Maybe." It was a logical conclusion. Occam's Razor—Annie's locket, Annie's key. "I don't remember ever seeing her wear it, though. Or talk about it. She talked about her grandmother all the time but never mentioned the locket."

"Would her mother know?"

"Sure. She'd know." Isabel hadn't talked to the Lewises since they'd left Gossamer Ridge after Annie's death. But Mrs. Lewis's sister still lived in Borland—surely she'd know where Mrs. Lewis was now. "I'll track down where Mrs. Lewis is now. But I can't help but believe Trey meant me to find whatever this key unlocks. Maybe he had proof the Swains were behind Annie's murder. Or some other evidence to bring them down."

"You're going to be busier working my case than I am."

"It won't be as dangerous for me, though." She touched his knee. "I wish I could check on you, make sure you're okay."

He looked pained. "We can't risk regular contact."

"Okay. But if you need me, find a way to reach me."

"I will," he promised.

She squeezed his knee. "What time are you supposed to be at the feed store this afternoon?"

"Around one. Addie said she wanted to give me a little orientation before she left for the barbecue."

"Orientation?" That didn't sound good.

"Not sure what that means, either," he admitted. "Maybe she'll just show me how to run the cash register or something."

She placed the key between the wings of the locket and snapped it shut, then fastened the chain around her neck. "Did Brand tell you what time the extraction team is coming for me?"

"We'll meet the agents at eight-thirty."

They fell silent. Isabel didn't know what Scanlon was thinking about, but her mind was racing through a dozen different scenarios that all seemed to end the same way: Scanlon dead and Isabel grieving him.

So many ways his investigation here could go wrong. So many places the Swains could hide his body where it might never be found. So many ways he could exit her life again, permanently, and not a damned thing she could do about it.

She'd been living the nightmare of losing Scanlon for six months already. It had felt like a bleak eternity.

How could she bear it for a lifetime?

AFTER A SHOWER, ISABEL had spent her morning cleaning up the cabin, her restless energy exhausting to watch. Scanlon had tried to tell her to leave things be, but she just told him to mind his own business.

"It's keeping me from going insane," she'd said, moving him out of the way so she could tackle the kitchen sink.

So he backed off and let her work, while he gave some thought about just how armed he needed to be for his afternoon at Tolliver Feed and Seed.

The problem with Halloran County was that the place was run, for all intents and purposes, by the Swain family. The sheriff was a Creavey, and most of his handful of deputies were either Swain cousins or extended family members of the non-Swains who helped run the methamphetamine production and marijuana farming operations.

The town of Bolen Bluff wasn't even incorporated, so what little government existed came by way of the Halloran County Commission, which consisted of three Swain relations and an outsider so cowed by the Swains that he usually skipped the commission meetings altogether. Might as well, since anything the Swains wanted to do would be passed, and anything they objected to would be voted down anyway.

"They've kept things how they want it by staying small," Scanlon explained to Isabel, as he finished dressing for his afternoon at Tolliver Feed and Seed. "They don't transport much out of this general area, at least not directly. They don't go after outsiders as a rule, and the Alabama Bureau of Investigation has too much on its plate to worry too much about local thugs killing other local thugs."

"Then why are they so suspicious that you could be a fed?" She held out her hand out for the comb he'd just picked up from the dresser and motioned for him to sit on the edge of the bed.

He let her comb his hair while he answered. "They're always suspicious. If they weren't worried I'm a fed, they'd be worried I'm from a rival operation the next county over, looking to horn in on their territory."

"I wonder why one of them would become a bomber for hire, then," she murmured, her expression intent as she groomed him.

"If it's J. T. Swain setting the bombs, he may have done it in conjunction with the SSU rather than his family business."

She stepped back to take a look at her handiwork. "Hate to admit this, Scanlon, but I think I like your hair a little longer. The scruff isn't bad, either."

He made a face. "It's harder to keep the scruff neat than it is to just shave. But I don't want to be recognized."

"Who'd recognize you here?"

He mentally chided himself for the slipup. "Nobody. I just meant if anyone who knows me happened to pass through. Which isn't likely to happen, since nobody just passes through Bolen Bluff. If you're here, it's for a purpose."

"Maybe that's why they're so suspicious of you.

You chose to come here when Bolen Bluff is more the kind of place a person chooses to leave." She played with a strand of his hair in the front, trying to smooth it into place. "What story did you give them for why you came here?"

"Said I couldn't work at the sawmill anymore with my bad hand. Couldn't stick around Texas to be reminded that my woman had left me for another man."

"Poor sad sack." She stroked his face lightly. "No wonder Dahlia was all over you like glue. Women can be suckers for a fellow down on his luck."

"Is it working on you?" he asked lightly.

She smiled. "Nah. I know you too well for that kind of stuff to work on me."

He felt a stab of guilt in the center of his chest. There were many things about him that Isabel didn't know at all. Like the story of his first eight years of life, how he and his parents had lived right here in Bolen Bluff. How he'd gone to school with some of these very people, people who looked at him now and didn't remember the boy he'd been twenty-five years ago.

He'd changed a lot—he was one of those rare people who didn't look a thing like his childhood photos. Even with his hair cropped short and his face shaved clean, he looked very little like the round-faced boy with crooked teeth and glasses who'd been the butt of every joke at Halloran County Elementary.

Strangely enough, it had been a Swain relation who'd been his only friend. Jamie had been a skinny, freckle-faced redhead who should have been the butt of a few jokes himself. Only later, when he understood the influence of the Swains on Halloran County, had Scanlon realized just why Jamie had escaped the teasing and bullying.

Scanlon hadn't seen his friend around Bolen Bluff since he'd been back. He hoped Jamie had escaped before this place had corrupted him completely.

"Okay, you look presentable." Isabel set the comb on the dresser. "Do you have any idea what you'll be doing today at the feed store?"

"If I'm lucky, I'll get a chance to snoop around a little."

"They might have some sort of surveillance set up—"

"No," he said firmly. "This much I know about the Swains—they eschew technology like that. Too afraid it might fall into other people's hands and reveal their own crimes. They do their surveillance the old-fashioned way—break in while you're not home and snoop, or else station someone nearby to watch your every move. Hopefully, they've come to trust me enough not to put someone there at the shop to watch me."

Isabel frowned. "Promise you'll be careful, Scanlon. Don't get overconfident. This is more likely a test of your intentions than a show of faith on their part."

"I know. Believe me." He stood and crossed to where she leaned against the dresser. "I'll be back here before you know it, Cooper."

"And then it'll be time to say goodbye." She looked so sad it made his own gut tighten with pain.

"It's better this way. You know it is. And you can follow up on that key. Maybe you'll find a way to connect the Swains to the bombing that killed your friend. It could bring their whole operation crashing down on top of them."

"And send you back to D.C. to the FBI."

He stroked her hair, quelling the fierce urge to kiss her. "The FBI will take you back. You know they will. It could be just like before."

She shook her head. "It can't go back to the way it was before. Not after last night." She looked up at him, as if trying to read his thoughts. He kept his expression guardedly neutral, not ready to commit to anything outside of the emotional status quo he'd maintained for so long.

He had never let himself get involved in long-term relationships while working for the FBI. He'd told himself it was because he didn't have the time or energy to devote to someone outside of his job. But how much of his reluctance came from his desire to devote every available second to his quest to find his father's murderers?

And how much of it, asked a quiet voice in his head, *was that those other women you dated weren't Isabel Cooper?*

He had to leave the cabin at twelve-thirty in order to be early for his one o'clock appointment with Addie Tolliver. Isabel walked him to the front door of the cabin and rose to her tiptoes, stopping him from opening the door. "Remember what's waiting here for you if you manage to come back safe and sound," she whispered before kissing him so thoroughly his whole body hummed like a tuning fork.

He made it to the cab of the truck and belted himself in, glancing toward the front of the cabin. He couldn't see her in the reflective windowpanes, but he felt certain she was standing just inside, watching him leave through the narrow space between the curtains.

He felt the pull of her as surely as he could feel his own heart pounding a cadence of regret in his chest.

IF IT HADN'T MEANT SAYING goodbye to Scanlon for God only knew how long, Isabel would have been eager to get out of this cabin and back into the world. She felt stifled by the forced inactivity, the limited confines of the cabin's walls and, for the most part, Scanlon's bedroom.

There were too many memories in this particular room, she thought, her gaze drifting helplessly to the bed where she and Scanlon had made love the night before.

It had been everything she'd imagined it would be—passionate, thrilling, joyous and even sweet at times. Thinking about how often they'd denied themselves that pleasure in the past made her want to throw things. Breakable things.

When the clock clicked past one—the time when Scanlon's shift at the feed store started—she realized she had to find some way to occupy her restless mind or she'd go mad. She'd been reading the files in the portfolio Scanlon had put together until the lines seemed to run together, but outside of the locket revelation that had come from finding Trey Pritchard's name in the files, she'd learned nothing new.

Scanlon hadn't said she couldn't use the laptop computer while he was gone, had he? Maybe she could ping one of her siblings and see what was happening in Chickasaw County.

She moved aside the loose floorboard in the closet and retrieved the laptop and the smartphone. But as she was pulling them out of the small opening, the smartphone bumped the floorboard and skittered out of her hand, sliding deeper into the hiding spot.

"Damn it!" She set the laptop on the floor beside her and leaned down to reach farther into the cubbyhole. Her fingers brushed against something hard inside, but when she wrapped her fingers around the object, it was larger and heavier than a phone. She tugged it out of the hole and discovered she was holding a clear flat plastic storage box about the size of a thick notebook. Inside lay a thick stack of papers.

She unsnapped the fastener that held the box closed and looked through the papers inside, her brow furrowing as she saw that most of the pages were photocopies of newspaper articles from twenty-five years ago, from a variety of different Alabama newspapers. But they all detailed the same story: a sheriff named Bennett Allen had been gunned down in his own driveway in the tiny Alabama town of Bolen Bluff.

Bennett Allen, Isabel remembered. That had been the name of the sheriff who'd taken a barrage of bullets not long after he'd put Jasper Swain behind bars.

She'd come across Allen's story while trying to connect the recent bombings to Jasper Swain through the bomb signatures, but she hadn't dug much deeper. Bennett Allen had died by gunfire, not a bomb. He had been a footnote in her research, not a focus.

But apparently to Scanlon, Bennett Allen had become more than a focus, she realized as she flipped through the papers and discovered they all had something to do with Bennett Allen's murder. His death was apparently an obsession.

There were old autopsy reports, ballistics, evidence lists, crime scene notes—everything a detective might have pulled together if he were attempting to solve a cold case.

Was Scanlon trying to find Bennett Allen's murderer? Was that the real reason he'd agreed to go undercover in the midst of the Swains?

She set the plastic box aside just long enough to retrieve the fallen cell phone, then grabbed the box, the phone and the laptop and carried them all into Scanlon's bedroom. Setting up in the center of the bed, she powered up the laptop and typed Bennett Allen's name into the web search engine.

She kept narrowing her search until she found just a handful of mentions, mostly posthumous. One of the more informative of the bunch came from a website run by Appalachi-Watch, a nonprofit, self-styled anticrime watchdog focused on aggregating stories of drug smuggling among the poor and insular mountain clans who still lived in parts of the Appalachian Mountains.

Even their mention of Bennett Allen was mostly cursory—a rather overwrought obituary to the man's bravery in bringing down the head of the Swain crime family. The account included the heartbreaking detail that Allen was murdered in front of his eight-year-old son, Bennett Allen Jr.

The hair on the back of Isabel's neck prickled. *Bennett Allen Jr.* Ben Allen Scanlon was Scanlon's full name. With the "Allen" spelled just like that.

Son of a—

She went back through the newspaper accounts, looking for details. One of them, an article from the Fort Payne *Times Journal,* included a photograph taken at the sheriff's funeral. The shot was focused on a young boy of eight, with dark, buzz-cut hair and light-colored eyes gazing seriously at the camera through a pair of horn-rimmed glasses. If he had been in the photograph alone, Isabel didn't know if she'd have recognized her partner.

But the woman standing next to him, holding his hand and weeping, was definitely Scanlon's mother, Reva. She had aged well over the twenty-five years since her first husband's murder. She hadn't looked much different the last time Isabel had seen her, standing at the graveside while they said goodbye to whatever pile of dust SAC Adam Brand had arrange to be buried in Scanlon's place.

Isabel closed her eyes, overwhelmed by a contradiction of emotions. Sadness for her partner, who'd lost his father in a horrible way, right in front of his eyes. Anger that he had been her partner—her best friend—for seven years and never once let on that the man he called Dad was his stepfather.

And fear. Perhaps fear most of all. Because if Scanlon hadn't told her this one most vital of details about his life, what else had he been keeping from her? Was everything she thought she knew about him a lie as well?

Chapter Fifteen

The sounds of the barbecue filtered through the open door of Tolliver Feed and Seed, drawing Scanlon's attention toward the street, where bright daylight washed out Main Street until it looked like a skeleton bleaching in the sun. Addie Tolliver had been lucky; the day of Leamon's birthday party had turned out to be sunny and warm, with temperatures rising into the low eighties by early afternoon. Most of the townsfolk who drifted past the feed store were dressed in shirtsleeves and shorts, even some of the men.

There would be a few folks in town who refused to make an appearance, but they were outsiders in Bolen Bluff now, no matter how long their families might have lived here. The Swain family owned the town, like it or not.

Addie hadn't given him many instructions before she headed out to the party, perhaps because she knew that anyone who might have wanted to shop today would be at the party. He didn't know whether or not her invitation to fill in this afternoon was an overture, as he'd hoped, or just a sign that Addie knew any warm body holding down the fort would do.

Davy had said a bluegrass family was coming in to town to play for the event, and sure enough, Scanlon could hear the sound of banjos, fiddles and mandolins wafting in on the warm breeze, pounding out a lively reel.

One of the mysteries of the Swains' criminal enterprise, to Scanlon at least, was where the money actually went. No telling how much drug cash the family laundered through the feed store every year, yet the place was as shabby as any general store a man might find in any tiny Southern hamlet. The tile floors were clean but worn, the painted metal shelves chipped and warped in more places than not.

Scanlon wished he dared go to the back room for a look, but he couldn't be sure he wasn't being watched. Hell, Addie might have stationed one of her boys in the back room to catch him in the act if he had a mind to go snooping.

This was a test. One he had to pass to get any deeper into the family business. So he had to keep his nose clean.

Still, by the time a half hour had passed, boredom was beginning to set in with a vengeance. He decided to leave the narrow confines of the cashier's counter and walk up and down the feed store's aisles to work off some of his restless energy.

He had just turned up the goat feed aisle when

saw that he was no longer alone in the store. Three men stood silhouetted in the doorway, backlit by the brilliant daylight. Scanlon had to walk all the way up to where they stood before he could make out any features. What he saw when he reached the front made his pulse notch up a couple of levels.

Two of the men were Nolan Alvarez and Toby Lavelle, aka Norman Bayliss and Jeff Munroe, the SSU agents he'd met earlier in the woods by the river. The other man was more slight, with distinctly Asian features.

Kurasawa? Scanlon wondered.

"Addie Tolliver's letting us drop off a shipment." Alvarez didn't even pretend to be the harmless fisherman he'd posed as the last time they'd met. "We're supposed to store it in the back room."

Was this part of the test, too? Scanlon weighed his options. If he used the handheld radio Addie had left with him to contact her, she might be mad as hell at being interrupted at the family party. But let these guys stash their goods in the back room without permission, and Addie would definitely see his presumption as a big black mark against him.

"Mrs. Tolliver didn't mention you'd be coming," he said, infusing his voice with doubt but not much curiosity. At their darkening expressions, he added, "I can call her up on the two-way, though." He pulled the radio from his pocket and showed it to them. At Lavelle's sharp gesture of command, Scanlon thumbed the talk button. "Mrs. Tolliver?"

A few seconds later, Addie Tolliver's voice came over the radio, tight with annoyance. She had to speak over the bluegrass band's toe-tapping rendition of "Bonaparte's Retreat." "This better be good, Mr. Shipley."

Scanlon told her about the unexpected visitors and their request, taking care to play up his nervousness. If nothing else, it might make the SSU agents and the gunrunner drop their guard a bit. "Should I let them in?"

"I forgot to tell you they was coming," Addie said, her tone utterly unconvincing. So he'd been right—this was part of the test. "Take them on into the back. They're selling me some surplus stock from a store over in Perry, Georgia, that went belly up. Damned economy."

"Okay, ma'am. I'll take care of it." Scanlon pocketed the radio and nodded to the men. "She said I should show you the way to the back."

The two former SSU agents just smiled, but Kurasawa seemed annoyed. He complained about the delay to the two men in rapid-fire Spanish. His accent was definitely South American rather than Mexican, which lent more credence to Rick Cooper's theory that this Kurasawa might be a Peruvian gunrunner. The size and shape of the boxes the three men unloaded from a flatbed truck parked outside—long, rectangular boxes that would be perfect for carrying rifles or even RPGs—rocket-propelled grenade launchers—only added more evidence to the theory.

The men seemed loath to leave him alone with their goods in the storeroom, but they finally left after pretending interest in the hardware section of the store. Scanlon tried not to react with relief, still aware he could be under surveillance.

The temptation to head back to the storeroom and see what, exactly, might be in those boxes was strong. But that was what Addie and the boys might expect a federal agent to do. Scanlon wasn't a federal agent around here. He was Mark Shipley, a down-on-his-luck ex-vet looking for enough money to keep food on the table and a roof over his head, and not too particular about how that money ended up in his pocket.

What would Mark Shipley do? He'd keep his eyes averted and his mouth closed.

But it took every ounce of effort he possessed to stick close to the register until Addie Tolliver and her son Leamon returned near the end of the day.

Both of them were flushed and laughing, the day's heat accounting for only a small amount of their pink cheeks and lifted moods. The smell of corn mash was strong on Leamon's breath, especially.

He dropped a paper plate covered with plastic wrap on the counter. "Davy said he promised you some food to take home," Leamon said, sounding a little peeved. "Wasn't a whole lot left after everyone got through, but you ought to be able to get a nice meal out of that."

Scanlon thanked him, ignoring Leamon's grimace. He turned to Addie, who was swaying side to side as if listening to a reel in her head. "Mrs. Tolliver, I sure do thank you for the chance to work. You keep me in mind if you need someone to fill in again, you hear?"

Addie's blue eyes slid into focus, settling on his face. "I reckon you'll be wantin' your pay now, too." She went around to the cash register, swaying slightly on unsteady legs, and pulled a twenty out of the drawer. "Consider the two dollars a bonus for your good work," she said with a tipsy smile, a phantom of the pretty girl she once must have been making a brief appearance.

Scanlon thanked her again and carefully balanced the plate of leftovers in one hand as he headed out the door. On the drive back up the mountain to his cabin, his eagerness to get to the satellite phone to call Adam Brand made his driving foot heavier than ever. He forced himself to slow the truck to more normal speeds. The mountain roads could be treacherous, even in broad daylight.

He checked the filament he'd left on the door as an early warning. It was in place, completely intact, so he let himself inside and called Isabel's name.

"Back here," she called, her voice flat and brisk.

He followed the sound and found her in the bedroom, sitting on the edge of the bed, her gaze directed toward the window. Her rigid spine and jutted chin sent a tremor darting through his belly. He knew the signs. She was angry.

A second look at the bed told him why. Sitting next to her, the lid open to reveal the contents, was the plastic box where he kept his notes on his father's murder.

How the hell had she found it? He'd hidden it deep inside the shallow cubbyhole where he stored his other secrets, well beyond easy discovery.

"Never took you for a snoop, Cooper." As soon as the defensive words came out of his mouth, he regretted them, even before she turned her furious dark gaze on him.

"The phone slipped out of my grasp," she said in a tight, furious tone. "I had to feel around in the hole to find it and came across this." She thumped the box. "I have to wonder why you hid it from me as if it was your porno stash or something."

"I don't have a porno stash—"

Her gaze whipped up again, positively lethal. "Seven years, Scanlon. I've had your stupid back for seven years, risking my life and my sanity for you, and all you've done the whole time is lie to me."

"It wasn't all lies," he protested.

"But it was the big one." She reached into the storage box, her fingers ruffling the pages inside. "A whole life I didn't know a damned thing about."

He wasn't sure if she was talking about his short

life as Bennett Allen Jr. or the secret life he'd lived obsessing over his father's death.

"Did it ever occur to you that I could have helped you?" Her voice came out almost plaintive. "I'm a good investigator. If you'd just told me the truth—"

The skin on his neck crawled at the thought. His life as Bennett Allen Jr. was a secret, even in his family. His mother had moved them out of Alabama not merely out of grief but also fear. Fear that he'd remember who fired the shot that night. Fear that whoever had killed his father would decide he was a risk they couldn't afford to leave alive.

"You're Ben Scanlon," his mother had told him soon after she married a very kind man who'd been more than happy to adopt her son and give him a new name. "George is your daddy now."

The other life, didn't—couldn't—exist. Except in his memory, and now in the secret world that came alive only when he opened that plastic storage box.

Isabel's expression shifted, puzzlement showing in her eyes. "Are you afraid to talk about it?"

He crossed to the bed and sat next to her, looking down at the stack of papers that constituted the only things left of his former life. "My mother believed I'd be killed if we stayed around. I saw who did it. As far as he knew, I could testify against him."

"So you know who did it?"

He shook his head. "I don't remember. I never do. Sometimes I dream about it, but the movie in my brain always skips that scene and goes right into the aftermath. I hear the truck. The gunshot. I see Daddy lying in his own blood—"

Her voice softened. "But nothing else?"

He shook his head. "I've tried hypnosis, therapy—I've tried everything out there. But I just can't remember that one moment of time."

Her soft fingers brushed lightly over his. Just one light touch before she withdrew her hand again. He felt a chasm still stretching out between them, impossible to cross.

How had they gone so quickly from this morning's intimacy to this afternoon's distance? By one small lie?

But it wasn't a small lie. It was huge. He'd lied about who he was, about a vital part of his life he'd hidden from everyone else in the world—including her.

He scrubbed his burning eyes with the heels of his palms. "I'm sorry."

"That you lied or that I found out about it?"

Her flat tone made him wince. He gave her the honesty she deserved. "That you found out about it."

She was silent for a long moment. Then she sighed. "How'd the shift at the feed store go?"

He'd almost forgotten all about his encounter with the SSU agents and their gunrunning buddy Kurasawa. Quickly, he outlined what had happened. "I'm not sure it's the start of an actual gunrunning venture or a test."

"Maybe it's both," Isabel suggested.

"Maybe." He noticed for the first time that the knapsack he'd retrieved from the drop site that first night was sitting on the floor by the bed. It looked full. "You're already packed to leave?"

"Didn't see the point of waiting 'til the last minute."

He glanced at the bedside alarm clock. It was half past six already. "Have you eaten any dinner?"

"No."

"Come on. One last bologna sandwich for the road."

The look she shot him was full of exasperation, but he saw a little softening, too. He'd take it. He didn't want her to leave him—possibly forever— still hating his guts.

"I lied about the bologna," he said when they reached the kitchen, showing her the leftovers he'd brought home with him.

"Are you sure Leamon Tolliver didn't poison it?" she asked doubtfully, as she sat down across from him at the card table.

"Davy McCoy better hope not," Scanlon said with a grin. "I ran into him on the way to my truck and traded the plate Leamon gave me for the one Davy had. Davy was so drunk he didn't even notice the switch."

"You're so bad," she murmured, but he saw a hint of a smile at the corner of her lips.

A fresh ache of regret washed through him. Two hours. That was all he had left with her now, and he was wasting most of it trying to fix the damage done by his lifetime of lies.

"I should have told you," he admitted. "I knew six months into working together that you were the soul of honesty and discretion. You'd have never said or done anything that would put me in danger or set me at odds with our bosses."

"So why didn't you tell me?"

"Habit, I guess," he answered slowly, trying to sort through motives he'd never bothered to examine before now. "Maybe a little shame."

"Shame? For what?"

He spooned half of the leftovers onto the clean paper plate in front of her. "For not remembering who killed my father."

"You were a little boy and it was a huge trauma."

"If I'd just remembered, I might not be here now." He reached across the table and touched the locket hanging around her neck. "Your friend might even be alive, if the same person who killed my father was behind the bomb that killed your friend. You wouldn't be a target."

"You don't know that the shooter and the bomber were the same person."

"I don't know that they weren't."

"You think it was a Swain."

"I'm certain it was a Swain. I just don't know which one."

She pushed the sauce-slathered barbecue pork around the paper plate without actually eating any of it. "I read through all the articles while you were gone."

"What did you learn?"

"Very little," she admitted. "Now that I know you don't remember what happened, I'm curious why not. Did your dad knock you to the ground to protect you and you hit your head, maybe?"

"No. It happened too fast for that. I think the shots came before either one of us realized what happened."

"Maybe you jumped out of the way and ended up taking a knock on the head from that."

"No, I remember one thing very clearly. I was standing on my feet, looking down at my daddy's body in the driveway." The image was brutally clear in his mind, even now. "He'd taken two rounds in the chest. Rifle shots."

"Two .30 Winchester Center Fire cartridges," she murmured.

He nodded. "Left big holes."

"I'm sorry. That's a horrible picture to have in your head as your last memory of your dad." She closed her hand over the top of his. "Have you considered that the reason you can't remember the shooting is that you knew the shooter?"

"I'm pretty sure I knew him," he agreed. "Bolen Bluff's a tiny place, and I spent the first eight years of my life here, going to church and school, going downtown to eat dinner at the diner—" The diner wasn't there anymore, at least not the diner of his childhood. The Creavey family had taken it over at some point since he and his mother had left town for Texas. The former owners must have been one of the many families who'd fled town when the Swain family consolidated its hold on the place during the years right after his father's death. "I knew everybody back then."

"You don't look much like you did when you were a kid, but your mom looks almost exactly the same."

"George Scanlon's been good for her. He worked a nice, boring desk job for twenty-five years, came home at a decent hour and treated her like a treasure." He smiled, thinking about his stepfather. "He's been a good dad to me, too."

"He adopted you?"

"Yeah. That added another layer of protection to me, too. But he'd have wanted to do it, anyway."

"Does he know you witnessed your father's death?"

"Yeah. Mom told him. He's guarded our secret for decades now." Scanlon felt a rush of love for the man who'd made his mother smile again after his father's death. "If I'm honest with myself, I have to admit he's probably been a better husband than my own dad could have ever been for her. She doesn't constantly worry that when he walks out of the house in the morning he might never come back."

The satellite phone sitting on the table next to his untouched plate rang, sending a jolt of adrenaline through his tense body. He answered. "Yeah?"

"We're moving up the extraction time." It was Adam Brand. "Can you get her there at seven-thirty?"

"Yeah—but why the change?"

"Huntsville SAC needs his men back by ten for an operation they've had to set up last-minute. Trying to extract her at eight-thirty cuts things too close."

"Okay, we'll be there." He hung up and looked at Isabel, overwhelmed by the sense of time passing at the pace of a lightning strike. He saw an answering dread in her eyes.

"Your extraction time's moved up. We have to have you there at seven-thirty."

She closed her eyes briefly, then looked up at him again, her chin squaring with determination. "Better get a move on."

He followed her back to the bedroom to retrieve her things, acutely aware that the next half hour might be the last time they would ever get to spend together.

Chapter Sixteen

The ride in the back of Scanlon's old pickup truck wasn't as bad as it would have been had Isabel not been wrapped up snug as a bedbug in a thick quilt that hid her from view of anyone who might pass them by on their way down the mountain.

The truck rolled to a stop, the engine dying with a sputter. She felt a tug on the quilt. "Roll," came Scanlon's terse order, muffled by the layers of batting.

She started rolling, as they'd practiced, until she was free. Scanlon caught her as she nearly rolled off the open tailgate to the ground below. He kept his arms around her, his voice low in her ear as he asked, "You okay?"

"Fine," she answered, although her pulse was too rapid for comfort. She was standing in the middle of a small barn, little more than a shed, really, that might have housed a couple of horses, tops, in its heyday. But the time-faded wooden walls provided some cover for anything going on inside, while she suspected its exterior was nothing special enough to draw the attention of eyes well used to the sight of abandoned sheds, cabins and barns dotting the rural countryside like a blight.

"What time is it?" she asked.

He consulted his watch. "Seven-twenty. They should be here any time now."

"How are they coming?"

"Panel van, just like the one I used to bring you here in the first place."

A flash of memory shot through her brain. A kiss, hot and fierce, impossible to forget despite the fuzzing effects of the drug coursing through her system at the time.

"You kissed me, outside the van," she murmured aloud.

"I was afraid they'd see us, so I pretended we were lovers necking in the parking lot," he admitted, smiling slightly.

She crooked her mouth. "There wasn't a whole lot of pretending going on, as I recall."

His smile expanded. "You were a little out of it."

"Not that much." She edged closer to him, not only for the warmth radiating from his body but for the sense of intimacy she felt slipping further and further away from them. "I wish we could go back to last night."

He laid his forehead against hers. "Me, too."

She lifted her hands to his face, stroking his scruffy beard. "Know what I'm going to hope?"

"What's that?"

"I'm going to hope the key in my locket opens a bus locker full of evidence against the Swains. Then you can get the hell out of this godforsaken town and we can start all over again."

"You really think it's possible to start over after seven years?" he asked softly, his tone melancholy.

"If necessary."

He mimicked her earlier caress, his hands warm and strong where they cupped her jaw. "Is it necessary?"

"Maybe not," she admitted, finding herself a lot more forgiving of his secret-keeping now that time between them was running out so rapidly. "Maybe we could start back at the beginning of last night instead."

"That sounds a lot better to me," he admitted.

"But no more secrets."

He didn't answer, and she felt a twinge of unease. Were there more secrets he hadn't yet shared? The one thing she knew about Scanlon was that he didn't make promises if he didn't think he could keep them.

And had she really told him all her secrets? She hadn't told him that she had spent the last seven years falling head over heels for him.

What would he say to that secret revealed? Had he been doing likewise? Or was last night an aberration, an oasis in a desert of death and danger? A memory to pack away for later when they were both alone again?

The chance to ask that question slipped through her hands as the sound of a vehicle approaching sent them behind the truck for cover. Only when a panel van—dark blue this time instead of green—entered the narrow opening of the barn and parked did they ease out from hiding to greet the two FBI agents who emerged from the van.

To her surprise, one of the two agents was her cousin Will Cooper. The last she'd heard, he was working out of the Rome, Georgia, resident agency. He also seemed to have packed on twenty pounds since the last time she'd seen him, all muscle. She greeted him with a hug. "Will, what on earth are you doing here?"

"Got transferred to Huntsville last week," he said with a grin. "Got wind of this operation and talked my way into it. I figured there's nobody better to watch a Cooper's back than another Cooper."

Isabel waved Scanlon over. "Scanlon, this is my cousin Will Cooper. Will, this is Ben Scanlon."

"Nice to finally meet you, Agent Scanlon." Will shook Scanlon's hand. "Thanks for watching Isabel's back. There are a whole lot of Coopers who're real grateful."

"Cooper knows I'll always have her back." Scanlon shot her a look that made her bones melt.

"We've got to head out." The other agent, an older man with a thick head full of salt-and-pepper hair, spoke in an urgent tone and tapped his watch.

Isabel turned back to Scanlon, overwhelmed by a

rush of panic. She wasn't ready to leave. God only knew how dangerous the next few months, even years, were going to be for him, and he didn't have anyone to watch his back but Adam Brand, who was hundreds of miles away.

"I'll be fine, Cooper. You know I'm a survivor. Cheated death, didn't I?"

"Death always comes back for another round," she warned, clutching his hands tightly in her own. "Don't let the old bastard sneak up on you."

"I don't know if I'll risk emailing you, so I've told Brand to keep you updated every week, so you don't worry about me too much."

She didn't think even an update every hour would keep her from worrying, but she wasn't going to burden Scanlon with her fears. He had enough on his plate.

He wrapped his arms around her waist, pulling her close. She was surprised when he ignored the presence of the other agents and bent his head for a long, slow kiss. "I can't ask you to wait for me, Cooper. I can't even promise I won't have to do things that'll break your heart—"

She put her fingers over his mouth. "If you sleep with Dahlia McCoy, you won't have to worry about the Swains killing you. I'll do it for them."

He grinned at her. "Duly noted."

She closed her eyes, her heart breaking. "I don't suppose you'd consider telling Brand you're done, quitting the FBI and coming home with me right now?"

Even in the dim interior of the darkened barn, she could see the pain glittering in his eyes. "You know I can't."

She knew. And now that she knew the truth about his relationship to Bennett Allen, she knew why. She had a feeling his obsession with finding his father's killer would always trump every other passion in his life.

Even his passion for her.

Maybe he was right. Maybe it didn't make sense for her to wait around for a man who might never love her enough to let go of his past.

He kissed her again, lightly this time. It felt final. A goodbye. "Be safe, Cooper." As she turned toward the van, he added softly, "Be happy."

She faltered for a second, overwhelmed with the temptation to run back to his arms and beg him one more time to come with her. But she knew he would say no again. And she had enough pride left to keep walking.

The panel van had no windows in the cargo area, just a bench seat with a lap belt to keep her from being bounced around the interior. She threaded the belt through the strap of her knapsack to keep it in place, as well, and buckled herself in, trying to ignore the worried looks her cousin Will was shooting her way from the front passenger seat.

It was over. No harm done, right? Somehow, she'd figure out a way to be okay again.

However long it took.

TIME WAS HER ENEMY. SHE knew the man calling himself Mark Shipley was on his way down to the old abandoned barn to hand his pretty little bed buddy off to his FBI handlers.

She'd known there was more to the man than he'd let on, hadn't she? An FBI agent, snooping around the hills and valleys of Halloran County. Wasn't that a kick in the teeth for Addie and the boys? Once they knew what she knew now, all sorts of hell would break loose, and there was no telling how all the pieces would eventually fall.

She planned to be there to pick up the pieces.

She was intrigued by what she'd overheard the woman say about her locket. Now she knew why the boys had been after her in the first place—they'd learned about the key. It must have been Trey Pritchard who'd left that mess of blood and hair on the floor of Dillon Creavey's hunting cabin up on Thunder Ridge.

Though an outsider, Trey had been eager to make money and hadn't seemed to care much how he made it, so the boys had been happy enough to let the boy play mule on some of the more dangerous runs, especially since Pritchard had been just as happy to be paid in drugs as money most of the time.

She could have warned them about the folly of trusting a meth head with their secrets.

So what had Trey had on the Swains? Files? Addie handwrote all the illegal transactions in her books—could Pritchard have made copies of the ledger? Something like that could easily be kept in a bus locker or small storage area.

She used her key to get inside the cabin, taking care to ease aside the filament Mr. FBI used to alert him to visitors while he was away. From what she'd overheard, he kept important items hidden under a loose board in the hall closet.

She found the board and moved it aside, wrinkling her nose as she stuck her arm into the musty hole beneath the floor.

She didn't find the satellite phone they'd talked about, but the laptop computer and smartphone were there.

She pulled them out and didn't bother taking them elsewhere to set them up—what she was looking for she could find in just a few seconds. A glance at her watch revealed that seven-thirty had come and gone, meaning she was working on borrowed time now.

"Robert Frost," she muttered aloud, remembering how they'd spoken the words together. So cute.

So nauseating.

She entered the password—one word, lowercase—and found the information she needed. After jotting it on a notepad she'd brought with her, she shut off the computer, slipped it and the phone back into the crawlspace, and dropped the board back in place, wincing as it made a loud thump.

She heard the sound of a truck coming up the gravel track. Hurrying, she slipped out, replacing the filament where she'd found it. She scooted around the back of the cabin and out of sight just before the old Ford lumbered into the yard.

She waited, breathless, as the truck engine rattled to a stop and the door creaked open. She felt the adrenaline rush of a close call and couldn't hold back a smile.

She was good at this. Better than any of the other hicks and degenerates trying to play their redneck mafia games.

She was tempted to stick around, listen to the man Isabel Cooper called Scanlon. Reminding herself to do a little digging into who Scanlon really was, she slipped silently into the woods, sliding her hand into the pocket of her jacket to reassure herself that the notepad with the information she'd jotted was still there.

She had plans to finalize. Preparations to make.

She'd gloat later, when everything finally went her way.

THE DRIVE FROM BOLEN BLUFF to the Cooper Security office in Maybridge took about an hour and ended in the familial equivalent of a gang tackle in the conference room, where all five of her siblings were waiting for her arrival.

Rick reached her first, wrapping her in a bear hug that might have crushed the rib cage of a smaller, more fragile woman. His wife, Amanda, pulled him away, giving Isabel a quick smile and a heartfelt welcome home. Then her sisters, Megan and Shannon, took their turns, followed by Wade and her oldest brother, Jesse, whose outward calm couldn't mask the look of relief and affection in his dark eyes.

"Catch us up," he said tersely, showing her to the chair at the head of the conference table. "Anything you can tell us."

She related everything she could remember since spotting the man she now knew was Bobby Rawlings lurking at the end of the hall of the Fort Payne hotel, skimming over information that might put Scanlon in danger if it ever got out, even inadvertently. She trusted her brothers and sisters with every fiber of her being, but some secrets weren't hers to tell.

"So you think this key Trey Pritchard left you in the locket is going to uncover evidence against the Swain family?" Jesse asked, his tone guarded. But she could see the skepticism lurking behind his watchful eyes.

"I know it sounds crazy and random," she admitted, as usual finding the coincidences and happenstances of the theory a little harder to sell without Scanlon and his uncanny knack for finding patterns in chaos.

But he'd seen the same connections she had, making her doubly sure she was right. Trey Pritchard had somehow found incriminating evidence against the Swain family and hidden it away—whether for insurance or in angry response to the murder of his sister, Isabel didn't know. And she was pretty sure Trey was no longer alive to fill in the blanks.

But as soon as she could extract herself from the family powwow, she promised herself, she was going on a treasure hunt, armed with a key and the certainty that if she could find the hiding place, and reveal its secrets, she just might be able to bring Scanlon home safely.

She didn't know what would happen after that. All the same pressures that had kept them from acting on their attraction hadn't gone away just because they'd given in to their desires. Even Scanlon's confession about his real identity had only raised new conflicts to deal with, hadn't it?

But at least if he was safely home, away from the constant dangers surrounding him in Bolen Bluff, they'd have time to work through all the questions that still stood between them.

It was up to her to give them both that chance.

THE FILAMENT ON THE DOOR was still in place, and the cabin was still and silent. Scanlon dropped the truck keys on the card table in the kitchen and sank into the chair. The place seemed large and cold now that Isabel was gone.

Empty.

The clock over the stove read eight-forty-five. Too early for bed, despite his exhaustion. He should be feeling hungry, given that he'd eaten almost nothing of the food he'd brought home from the barbecue, but the thought of food made him queasy.

Isabel would be back home by now. He'd spent the last hour driving around Bolen Bluff just to keep himself from chasing her down and begging her to stay. Even now, he wished he dared to call her. But the last thing he could risk was staying in contact with her. On the contrary, he had to pretend the last few days had never happened.

Erase his time with her from his memories.

Impossible, he knew. What they'd shared here in this shabby little cabin was something he'd never forget.

But at least he could erase her from this place.

Room by room, he searched for signs of her—unfolding the futon to make sure nothing had fallen through the cracks, checking the bathroom to see if she'd left any toiletries, looking under the bed for any sign of a forgotten sock or a stray pair of underwear. He found none of those things.

But what he did find was infinitely more disturbing.

As he was rising from his crouch to look beneath

the bed, his gaze glanced across something small and round attached to the side rail of the bed.

With a tug, he pulled the object free, his gut tightening to a knot. Pinched between his thumb and forefinger was a small listening device about the size of a dime.

Someone had bugged his cabin.

"How long could it have been there?" Adam Brand's deep voice was wary but not unduly alarmed. Scanlon wanted to throttle him for his unnatural calm.

"I did an electronic sweep the day I brought Isabel here—three days ago?" He scraped his hand through his hair, trying not to lose his cool. He hadn't destroyed the bug yet—not without talking to Brand—but he knew he couldn't risk making the call to his boss from inside the cabin. He was out in his truck, ducked low in case anyone was watching. "It was all clear then, so it had to have been inserted since then."

"Could Cooper have done it?" Brand asked.

"No!" He forced himself to lower his voice. "No. Of course not. Unless you think she somehow faked her abduction—"

"No, but maybe once she knew the danger you were in—"

Would she have put electronic surveillance on him? Maybe if she'd had the opportunity, he had to concede. He'd probably have done something very like that in her place, just to know if she needed his help. Hell, he wished he'd thought to put a listening device in her purse or something, just so he could hear her voice and know she was okay.

But when would she have had a chance to obtain a bug? She was stuck at his place with no ride out, and besides, there certainly was nowhere any closer than Fort Payne where she could find a listening device to purchase.

"She wouldn't have had a chance to go get a bug anywhere. I never left her alone that long."

"And she's been there in your house the whole time, right? So when would anyone else have had a chance to plant a bug?"

"Well, there was the time that guy broke in and she had to hide in the closet," he said, remembering the sight of the tall, lean stranger moving silently through the woods outside his bedroom window. "It wouldn't have taken long to slip a bug under the bed rail."

"What about the McCoy woman—didn't you tell me she broke in looking for the woman you supposedly had holed up in your cabin?" Brand asked.

"Possible, I guess." And if she'd been the culprit, he thought bleakly, she'd heard an earful the night he and Isabel had finally relieved seven years' worth of sexual tension.

He knew he should probably hope it was Dahlia

who'd planted the bug, but he thought he'd have a better chance surviving the wrath of the mysterious J. T. Swain.

"What could they have heard?" Brand asked.

Besides a few rounds of hot, pent-up sexual release? "Enough to put me in serious danger," he admitted. He told Brand about the discovery of the key inside the locket. "And we talked about my undercover assignment, more than once."

"Did you talk about your father's murder?"

For a second, Scanlon wasn't sure he'd understood the SAC correctly. Then a cold chill washed over him. "You know about my father?"

Brand sounded amused. "I know everything about my agents. Even things they try to hide from me."

Scanlon felt naked. "We did talk about my father, but not in a lot of detail." Not in the bedroom, anyway, which was the only place he'd found a listening device. "Not sure anyone who didn't already know who I am could have figured out the context of the conversation."

Brand was silent a moment. "Interesting that you're still kicking after all that."

"*Interesting* isn't the word I'd have chosen."

"Well, it may mean that whoever planted the bug hasn't been monitoring it in real time. It may just be recording somewhere." Brand sounded thoughtful. "Perhaps we can use that to our advantage."

"How?"

Brand's voice held a hint of wry humor. "Maybe it's time you go to Addie Tolliver and come clean about what you've been doing in Bolen Bluff all this time."

Chapter Seventeen

The bus station in Maybridge was little more than a hole in the wall on Main Street, not far from the post office. Most of the business that moved through the station was shipping; passengers were more likely to drive over to the bigger city of Borland in the next county over, a bus line hub. However, the small Maybridge office did offer storage lockers for the few passengers who caught buses as they came through town.

But there was no locker number 112.

Isabel muttered a soft curse, drawing a chuckle from her brother Wade, who'd insisted on joining her search mission.

"You never used to cuss before you joined the FBI."

"You were a Marine and you have the nerve to complain about my salty language?" she retorted before she realized that any mention of his former military service tended to make her brother melancholy.

He sighed. "Point taken."

She hooked her arm through his as they walked out into the unseasonably warm April sunshine. His limp was noticeable, and probably always would be. But Isabel remembered the hours he spent in agonizing limbo during and after the emergency surgery to replace his shattered knee. The round from the Kaziri rebel's Kalashnikov had destroyed his kneecap and broken all three bones in his right leg. Doctors later told the family that Wade was damned lucky they'd been able to save the leg at all.

"What's next—the station in Borland?"

"Gossamer Ridge is closer." As she slid behind the wheel of her Toyota FJ Cruiser, her BlackBerry made a soft beep. She checked her email and saw she had a new message from an M. Shipley. It took a second to remember that Mark Shipley had been Scanlon's cover identity.

She opened the mail. The message was terse. "Think I've found the lock for your key. Meet me at the drop, 11:00 am. Come alone—under extra scrutiny. Don't reply—shutting down now and can't check back."

"Something wrong?" Wade was looking at her with the same worried gaze that all her siblings seemed to share these days, ever since her return home.

"No," she said, opting not to tell him about the message. No way would anyone in her family let her go meet Scanlon alone, as he'd asked. They'd try to come up with some elaborate commando mission—

and probably find a good excuse to leave her back home under 24-hour protection.

To keep Wade from getting suspicious, she went along with him to the Gossamer Ridge bus station. After Scanlon's email, she wasn't too surprised when there was no locker number 112. Was Scanlon right? Had he found the lock that fit the key?

She wished she could email him back for more information. Was it strange that he'd told her not to? Of course, he'd told her he probably wouldn't want to contact her by email often.

A finger of unease played over the back of her neck as she silently considered the possibilities. When she'd left Scanlon in Bolen Bluff, his cover had still been solid. In fact, he'd been closer than ever to breaking through the wall separating him from the Swain drug operation.

Maybe the Swains had finally brought him into the business.

"On to Borland?" Wade asked when they returned to the SUV.

She glanced at the dashboard clock. Nine-fifteen—if she wanted to make it to Bolen Bluff before eleven, she had to leave soon. "No, let's take a break. I want to go over the files again to see if I missed any clues." Scanlon had arranged for Brand to overnight copies of the FBI's Swain-family-related files to Isabel. They'd arrived first thing that morning and were locked in the safe at her house.

She dropped Wade off at the Cooper Security

office and headed back home to the pretty little farmhouse she'd bought a few months earlier. She didn't bother with the files in the safe, however. After dressing in a pair of olive drab jeans and a camouflage T-shirt she'd permanently borrowed from her brother Jesse, she grabbed a lightweight backpack and shoved a couple of boxes of .38 and 9 mm ammunition inside, one for her Beretta and one for the Smith & Wesson .38 she strapped to her ankle as a backup weapon. At the last minute, she added a compact boot knife to her other ankle.

Just in case.

Rain was forecast for the midmorning, thunderstorms for the afternoon, along with a drop in temperatures, so she grabbed a jacket, as well. If she and Scanlon were lucky, they'd find what they were looking for long before the storms rolled in.

And if they were very lucky, the key in the locket around her neck would unlock enough damning evidence against the Swain family to put them all away for a long time.

The drive to Bolen Bluff seemed to drag forever, though she reached the bottom of Dogwood Ridge an hour early. She eased her SUV into the abandoned barn where she'd met the extraction team last night. The drop site was empty and still.

Taking care, she eased out of the Toyota and scanned the dim interior of the barn, using the flashlight on her key chain to examine all the gloomy corners. She saw nothing that looked like a booby trap or an ambush waiting to happen.

So why was every instinct she possessed screaming for her to get the hell out of there?

"YOU KNOW THERE'S AT LEAST a seventy percent chance I'm going to be shot dead before I can explain a damned thing, right?" Scanlon tucked the satellite phone under his chin and checked the clip of his Kel-Tec P-11 before he tucked it into the holster strapped at his ankle.

"You've lived through worse odds," Brand reminded him.

"Once."

"I can extract you now, if that's what you want."

Scanlon dropped his leg to the floor and slumped in the kitchen chair. Extraction was probably the smart option. The sane one. But if he got out now, he might never have another chance this good to find out who shot his father.

"It's not what I want," he growled.

Brand was silent on the other end of the line. Scanlon knew he had to be wondering, by now, why his formerly cautious agent had suddenly become gung-ho about dangerous undercover work. The SAC finally spoke in a low, careful tone. "Let's just keep it simple. Go to Addie—she's got the final word, and she's not going to feel as personally affronted by the lies as her boys will. Plus, she's not as hotheaded, either."

"Getting her alone could be the problem."

"You could call ahead."

"And give them time to set up an ambush? No."

"She's most likely at the feed store."

"That's what I figure, too." Scanlon shrugged on a denim jacket, even though he suspected he'd be sweating like a pig in a sauna after a few minutes in the humid heat outside. The jacket made him feel a little less vulnerable, as if the denim was an added layer of armor. It was ludicrous, of course—the jacket only added an extra layer of potential shrapnel that would blow through him if someone sent a bullet flying his way, but if he thought he was less vulnerable, maybe he'd behave that way.

It was going to take a show of bravado to pull this particular scam on Addie Tolliver.

The feed store didn't open on Sundays, officially, but Scanlon knew that was where Addie would be. She spent most days there, tending to the small shop as if it were her child. He suspected Leamon would agree—he'd been on the receiving end of more than one public dressing-down since Scanlon returned to Bolen Bluff. Nothing Leamon Tolliver did was ever good enough for his mother.

Leamon had seemed, at first, a promising choice for a double agent. But Scanlon had figured out, early on, that most of Addie Tolliver's complaints about her son were true. He was lazy and venal, and Scanlon was sure he'd be just as unreliable and uncontrollable an ally for the FBI as Addie found him to be for her own operation.

Scanlon tried the front door of the shop. Locked. Not necessarily a deterrent, though his lock-picking skills weren't quite up to his partner's. But first, he went around to the back and simply knocked, hoping Addie would answer.

Addie came to the door, peering out into the morning sunshine with a look of irritation on her square face. "Mr. Shipley. I reckon I wasn't exactly expecting you."

He could tell from the emphasis she put on his undercover name that she knew who he really was. "I suppose you weren't. But I think maybe we need to do a little talking."

Her leathery face cracked with a smile. "I reckon you're at a disadvantage, aren't you, G-man? Not much to offer me that I'd be in the market to buy."

"You haven't seen anywhere near all I have to offer," Scanlon shot back with a show of confidence, quelling the fear swelling in his gut. "May I come in?"

Addie stepped back, the smile on her face broadening.

Scanlon tamped down a flood of raw fear and entered the back of the store.

He wasn't all the way inside before a half dozen pairs of hands were on him, driving him facedown to the floor.

OVERHEAD, STORM CLOUDS smudged the sky. Isabel crouched low behind a kudzu-smothered shrub and tugged her camouflage jacket more tightly around her, glad she'd listened to the weather report and anticipated the dropping temperatures.

She'd moved the FJ Cruiser from the barn the minute her danger radar started pinging, parking it a half mile away behind a canopy of kudzu. Backtracking, she'd settled in to wait, hoping her instincts were wrong.

Hoping it would be Scanlon who next appeared on the dirt road leading up the mountain to his cabin.

She couldn't see much beyond her hiding place. She could hear, however. A vehicle was moving up the road toward her.

Unfortunately, it wasn't Scanlon's old Ford pickup. The engine noise was a purr, not a rattle.

The car stopped just before it moved into the narrow gap between bushes that would have afforded Isabel a clear view. She eased back deeper into cover and waited for the new arrival to make himself known.

Footsteps, quick and light, moved across the hardened dirt track. A woman, Isabel realized, just before her prey finally came into view. She bit back a gasp of surprise.

Dahlia McCoy.

The slender blonde checked her watch. Isabel took a quick peek at her own watch. Ten forty-five. She looked back up to see Dahlia slip inside the barn. Lying in wait for her arrival?

She would be exposed, briefly, if she crossed the road, but she needed to get closer, to peek through the gaps between the rotting boards of the barn to see what Dahlia was up to.

She took the chance and edged out of her hiding place, sticking close to the underbrush to take advantage of her camouflage clothing. Angling toward the corner of the barn, where it would be hardest for anyone inside to spot her movements, she moved silently across the dirt road and flattened herself against the weathered clapboard.

Inside, she heard movement. She dared a quick glance through a nearby gap in the wood siding, but the interior of the barn was too dark for her to make out anything. And now, out in the open, she was too exposed, in case Dahlia had any backup coming. But she didn't want to go back to the bushes and wait for something else to happen.

She needed to draw Dahlia out into the open.

But what if Scanlon were coming here to meet her? Dahlia's presence didn't mean the email was a hoax. Maybe Dahlia had somehow gotten wind of his plan to meet with Isabel and had decided to catch him in the act of cheating on her. Scanlon had seemed pretty sure that Dahlia had no connection to the Swain drug operation, so wasn't it more likely that her motives for snooping around were personal?

The sound of footsteps clicking across the hard

dirt floor inside the rickety structure made Isabel press herself flatter against the side of the barn. She eased her hand onto the Beretta holstered at her side and readied herself.

Dahlia emerged from the barn in a sudden rush, heading straight for Isabel. She held a rusty shovel in her hands and charged at her, swinging for her head.

Isabel dodged the blow, but the edge of the shovel caught the wrist of her gun hand as she brought the Beretta up to protect herself, slicing through the flesh and rattling the bones. The Beretta slipped from her numb fingers and hit the ground with a soft thud.

Isabel ignored the pain and reset herself, throwing out her leg to catch Dahlia as she tried to right herself to take another strike with the shovel. Dahlia sprawled forward, face-first, and Isabel threw herself on the woman's back, pinning her on the ground.

Dahlia's hands scrabbled forward toward the fallen Beretta, but Isabel caught her by the hair, jerking her head back. She pulled the Smith & Wesson from her ankle holster and pressed the barrel against the side of Dahlia's head. "Don't think I won't use this."

Dahlia drew her hand back, her breath coming in short, rapid gasps. "What are you going to do, kill me?"

"Why are you here?" she asked.

"Just walking through the woods," Dahlia said between ragged breaths. "I saw someone with a gun outside the barn, so I struck."

Isabel could tell the woman was lying. For one thing, she'd parked here deliberately at the drop site, a few minutes before the time indicated in the email purportedly from Scanlon. And there was a smug tone to her voice, as if she couldn't quite keep herself from letting Isabel know that she was aware of just who Isabel was.

But did she have any idea who Scanlon was?

Isabel was almost positive the Swains had targeted her because of the locket. That was how they'd identified her—Isabel Cooper, Annie Pritchard's friend and the girl to whom Trey had given the locket. Not Isabel Cooper, the FBI agent who'd been investigating the bombings that might be connected to the Swains. It was possible the Swains didn't even realize, yet, that the FBI had any interest in their operation.

So which Isabel Cooper had Dahlia come here to look for?

"I can't breathe," Dahlia groaned.

Isabel eased off the woman's back, but kept the barrel of the gun pressed against her head. She kicked the shovel aside, out of Dahlia's reach, and circled to retrieve the Beretta. Her hand was slick with blood, almost losing its grip on the weapon, but the shovel edge seemed to have missed any major blood vessels, for the blood flow had slowed and was already starting to clot.

"If you were just walking through the woods," Isabel said, glancing at the three-inch heels of Dahlia's brown leather pumps, "why the stilettos?"

"They make my calves look fabulous," Dahlia shot back, turning her head to glare at Isabel, ignoring the gun to her head. "You're not going to shoot me. You're one of the good guys, right?"

"How would you know that?"

Dahlia forced the issue, pulling away from the gun and sitting up so she could look at Isabel. "Let's not pretend we don't both know what's going on."

"What's going on?"

Dahlia smiled. "I want that locket."

Isabel arched an eyebrow at the direct approach. "Why?"

"I need the key inside."

"What makes you think I haven't used it already?" Isabel saw no point in pretending she didn't know what Dahlia was talking about.

"You'd know the email was fake—that Ben Scanlon couldn't have found the lock the key belongs to," Dahlia answered flatly. "You would have found a different way to contact him."

Isabel felt her blood chill. "Who?"

Dahlia laughed. "Oh, that's nothing, hon. I know his real name. Bennett Allen Jr." Her eyes glittered with bitter mirth. "Old Sheriff Allen's boy."

How had she found out? Had someone here in Bolen Bluff managed to recognize him, despite the changes in his appearance?

"I guess you're wondering how I know that."

Isabel didn't answer, keeping a watchful eye on the other woman, worried by how little anxiety she seemed to be showing, given that she was looking down the barrel of a Beretta.

"The Swains are practically Luddites, the way they live. Most of them wouldn't have cell phones if you paid them to carry one. The feed store doesn't even have a security camera—did you know that?"

"What are you getting at?"

"I own a cell phone. I own a PDA, a MacBook Pro and an iPad." Dahlia smiled. "I'm not afraid of technology."

"You planted a listening device at the cabin," Isabel murmured. "Or was it a camera?"

Dahlia made a show of shuddering. "Not a camera. Listening to the two of you go at it like sex-starved teenagers was bad enough."

Isabel felt queasy. "Why are you telling me this?"

"I'm not the only one who knows who Mark Shipley really is, you know." Dahlia made a show of checking her watch. "I reckon the Swains have had him for a half hour now." She met Isabel's horrified gaze, a smile playing over her pretty lips. "Wonder how long they'll toy with him before they get tired of playing and put a bullet in his head?"

SCANLON'S PULSE POUNDED a cadence of regret, drowning out even the soul-sucking fear of impending death.

He was no longer in the feed store, but the cotton coffee bean sack fastened to his head with duct tape kept him from discerning where his captors had taken him.

He had been in a vehicle for a while, the smell of exhaust mixed with the heady aroma of coffee beans making for a nauseating ride. Rough hands had moved him to the place where he sat now, strapped to a hard chair by more duct tape.

He had flexed his hands as they'd strapped him in, trying to afford himself some wiggle room to get free. So far, they hadn't found the penknife tucked into the hidden pouch he'd sewn into every pair of jeans he'd brought with him to Bolen Bluff. The knife wouldn't do him much good in a fight, but it would free him of his bonds in a heartbeat if he could get one hand free.

The silence that filled the space around him was oppressive, giving his racing mind more time for self-recriminations. He should have opted out the second he'd discovered he'd been made. To hell with the truth about what happened to his father—would his father have wanted him to take on a suicide mission just to find the truth?

One of the Swains killed his father. Even if he remembered what happened, all these years later, a halfway decent lawyer would probably get the perpetrator off.

Was that worth dying for?

And what about Isabel? She'd already mourned him once, only to have him return to her life like a walking, talking miracle. Was he supposed to be okay with her having to mourn him all over again, this time for real?

He was an idiot. A selfish, cruel bastard to put her through any of this. If he got out of this mess alive, he was going to find her and tell her the truth. All of it.

Including how damned much he loved her.

Something cold and hard brushed against the skin of his collarbone, making him flinch.

"Don't move now. This blade is sharp." The voice was male and almost musical. Very rural Southern, like the Swains, McCoys and Creaveys, but while there was something familiar about the voice, Scanlon knew he hadn't heard it before.

The blade sliced through the duct tape holding the burlap bag over his face. What had been a blur of lights and shapes through the cotton mask became a small front room, decorated with a surprisingly feminine touch. Chintz throw pillows on a dark green camelback sofa near the window. A fading Persian-style rug softened the footsteps of Scanlon's captor as he stepped back, looking down at Scanlon with a quizzical half smile. He was a tall, rawboned man about Scanlon's age, with wavy auburn hair and sharp blue eyes. For a moment, a memory played at the edge of Scanlon's mind before disappearing when the man spoke again.

"I'd never have known it was you," he said.

Scanlon followed his gut and went on offense himself. "J.T. Swain, I presume."

"I reckon I answer to that," the man said with a soft chuckle. "For the last twenty years or so, anyway."

Footsteps clacked lightly against the hardwood floor beyond the rug. Scanlon turned his head to see the newcomer and found himself looking at a face that had once been nearly as familiar to him as his own mother's. "Mrs. Butler," he whispered.

Opal Butler sat on the sofa facing him, her face softening slightly. "I wasn't sure you'd remember me. There's so much else you don't remember."

"What am I doing here?" he asked, his brain growing fuzzy with a sudden onslaught of conflicting information. Opal Butler had been his best friend's mother. He and Jamie had played at the Butler house all the time. Opal Butler had made the best pecan cookies he'd ever tasted.

Yet here he was, trussed like a turkey in her parlor. A rogue MacLear SSU mercenary played idly with the deadly curved blade of a hunting knife while smiling at Scanlon, as if he knew a secret Scanlon didn't.

Then he took a closer look at Swain and saw the obvious. The freckles, the coloring, the brilliant blue eyes might be old Jasper Swain to the core, but the shape of the nose, the curve of the jaw—he was Earl Butler's son. Jamie Butler.

Scanlon's best boyhood friend.

Chapter Eighteen

"How long have you known?" Scanlon asked, his voice coming out faint and hoarse.

"Since Dahlia McCoy came by with a recording she thought we might want to listen to." Opal Butler was the one who answered. "I've got to hand it to the girl—she's got more brains than any McCoy I've ever known. Real drive. I think we might be able to use her in this operation."

"If she doesn't try to stab you in the back first," Jamie said with a hard laugh. He crouched so that he was eye to eye with Scanlon. "I guess you followed in your daddy's footsteps after all, huh, Benny?"

"I guess you didn't."

"Oh, I did. At first." Jamie stood up. "But nobody decent was gonna give a Swain a chance."

"MacLear did."

"They figured they could control me with what they knew about the Swain family. They put me in SSU right away. Figured I'd have flexible ethics." His voice lowered a notch. "I guess I lived down to that expectation."

There, Scanlon thought. A hint of vulnerability. The Jamie Butler he'd known had idolized Scanlon's father. He seemed to regret the choices he'd made.

Maybe Scanlon could use that.

"I reckon Dahlia's got her hands on that key now," Opal said, pushing to her feet.

Scanlon's gaze whipped up. "What key?"

Opal shrugged a cardigan over her dark green blouse. "The key girlfriend number one is taking off girlfriend number two as we speak, sugar." She flashed him a quick smile. "I always knew you'd be a real heartbreaker, Benny Allen." She headed out the door, closing it behind her.

"What is she talking about?" Scanlon asked Jamie, his pulse hammering hard in his throat.

"Dahlia lured your pretty FBI partner up here. Pretended to be you and told her to come alone and bring the key."

So they knew everything. About the key, about his FBI connection, about his real identity—

So why hadn't they killed him yet? Was there something they needed from him?

The key, he thought. They needed the key first, in case Dahlia's trick didn't get Isabel up here as planned.

Please, Cooper, please be smart enough to see through it.

But if there was one thing he knew about Isabel Cooper, it was that she didn't turn her back on her partner. If she thought there was the slightest chance the message had come from him, she'd be here.

He just hoped she'd come prepared.

"You don't have a thing on me," Dahlia taunted, as Isabel headed for the barn door. "I could have you arrested for unlawful detention. Maybe even kidnapping."

Isabel turned in the doorway. "You tried to brain me with a shovel, and I didn't even have my gun out."

"Your word against mine."

"And who will they believe—the former FBI agent with all sorts of commendations, or the sister of a meth mechanic? Let's see—what could the answer be?" Isabel headed out of the barn where she'd left Dahlia trussed up and headed up the road to the cabin in hopes that Scanlon had left some indication of where he was going.

Meanwhile, she got on the phone and put in a call to her brother Rick, swiftly explaining where she was and what she was up to. He was appalled, as she'd known he would be, but he promised backup was on the way.

Next, she tried the last number she'd had for Adam Brand. To her surprise, he answered on the first ring. "Brand."

"It's Isabel Cooper. Where is Scanlon?"

"I can't tell you that—you know that—"

Anger flooded her chest. "You can and you'd better. Because the Swain family knows who he is—"

"I know. He found the bug in his bedroom. He thinks J. T. Swain planted it—"

"He's wrong. Dahlia McCoy did."

"So the Swains may not even know about him?" Brand sounded suddenly alarmed.

"Oh, they know—but if you know he was made, why the hell haven't you pulled him out of here already?"

"We were going to use it." As Brand outlined his outrageous plan to have Scanlon pretend to offer himself as a double agent, Isabel's rage grew.

"Are you both crazy?"

"He has his reasons—"

"Are you talking about his father's murder?" she asked, no longer caring what secrets Scanlon wanted to keep. His obsessions weren't hers. Her only compulsion, at this moment, was to keep the man she loved alive, even if he was willing to kill himself to get the answers he needed.

"You know?" Brand sounded surprised.

"Everybody knows now, including the Swains. None of them is going to believe he'd go double agent for the family that killed his father."

Brand swore softly. "I'm sending in backup."

"Do you know where he is?"

"He was going into town to find Addie—he seemed to think she'd be at the feed store, even though it's Sunday." Brand's voice lowered. "He should have been there an hour ago."

Fear squirming in her belly, Isabel stopped in the middle of the dirt track, wondering if she should go back, get her car and drive into town. "They wouldn't keep him there, would they?" she asked aloud, not sure she could trust her instincts, which were telling her to stay in the woods.

"No," Brand agreed.

"I'm going to his cabin," she said, moving forward again. "I left my set of the files at home, but I know there's a map of Swain territory in his files. I'm going to start with Davy McCoy—see if he gives a damn about his sister and what happens to her."

"I can't sanction your actions," Brand warned.

"Lucky for you, I don't work for you anymore." Isabel hung up the phone and moved off the track and into the cover of the trees. As long as she stayed where she could see the road now and then, she knew she'd eventually reach the clearing where Scanlon's cabin was located.

But she didn't count on coming across another person there in the woods.

The woman was tall and large-framed, with graying red hair that curled wildly in the prestorm humidity. Her sharp blue eyes caught sight of Isabel before Isabel had a chance to hide, so Isabel lifted her chin and moved forward, pasting a smile on her face.

"Hi, there!" she called out, hoping her open greeting would disarm the woman enough to ease any suspicions she might have.

The woman tucked her cardigan more tightly around her and stepped forward, her freckled face creasing with a smile so predatory it made Isabel's skin crawl. "Well, hello yourself, Miss. You sure are out here wanderin' around at a bad time. There's a storm comin'."

"I know. I heard the hiking was good up here on the mountain, but I got turned around and my compass is a piece of garbage—don't suppose you could point me to the nearest road?"

"You're not far off—there's a dirt road just over that way that leads down to the highway into Bolen Bluff." The woman's eyes narrowed. "Is that where you're stayin'?"

"No, ma'am," Isabel answered, knowing that the one place she didn't want to go was back down the road to Bolen Bluff, especially if the woman decided to tag along. She'd tied up Dahlia McCoy pretty tightly, but she hadn't gagged her. "I came over the mountain from east of here—over in Silorville. My friends and I have been camping down by the lake."

"Good grief, girl, you're a long way off." The woman's eyes narrowed. "I could show you the path over the mountain if you like."

"Come into my parlor," said the spider to the fly....

"Okay," Isabel blurted before she lost her nerve.

"That'd be great." She fell into step with the larger woman, taking care to keep the Beretta holstered at her hip from showing beneath the hem of her camouflage jacket. All it had taken was the woman's mirthless smile to realize whoever she might be, she knew exactly who Isabel was.

Was she a Swain? Almost had to be—she didn't look exactly like Jasper Swain, whose mug shot Isabel had memorized, but they shared enough features in common—the freckled complexion, the red hair and rangy build—to make her feel certain this woman was, if not one of Jasper's sisters, at least a cousin.

Dillon Creavey's mother, perhaps? She definitely wasn't Addie Tolliver. Scanlon had a candid shot of Addie in his notes, and Addie was leaner and older than this woman. Addie also wore her hair in a short, wavy bob considerably shorter than her companion's shoulder-length frizz of curls.

Whoever she was, she seemed to know where she wanted to take Isabel. And it wasn't over the mountain to Silorville, which lay well west of wherever this woman was leading her.

"I'm Izzy," she introduced herself, using the annoying nickname her brothers and sisters sometimes used if they were in the mood to pester.

"Opal," the woman answered briskly, moving up the incline at a remarkably fast pace for a woman her size and age. "Nice to meet you," she added, almost as an afterthought.

Opal Butler. Old Jasper Swain's sister. Scanlon thought she and her sister Melinda never dabbled in the family business, but Isabel's instincts said otherwise. This woman was up to no good. Probably taking her wherever Scanlon was being held so the Swains could deal with both of them at the same time.

At least, that was what Isabel was counting on.

"WHAT HAPPENED TO YOU, man?" Scanlon kept a watchful eye on Jamie Butler as his old friend paced silently in front of the windows.

Jamie stopped and turned to look at him, anger and regret twisting in his sharp gaze. "You still don't remember, do you?"

Scanlon was beginning to. Pieces at a time. He remembered the sound of the truck engine as it chugged up the road by his house. It was blue—like Jamie's father's truck. Had Earl Butler killed Scanlon's father? Was that what he couldn't remember?

"It was cold that night. Damned cold. My fingers felt like they would freeze off, even under the gloves." Jamie resumed his pacing.

"You were there?"

"Of course I was there." He shot Scanlon a black look. "You know I was there."

A memory flashed through Scanlon's mind. Jamie's face, freckled and tearstained. Soft sobs audible in the crisp night air, even over the growl of the truck's engine.

The glint of moonlight on a rifle barrel as it settled over the frame of the open window.

No, Mama, please—

Bile burned in Scanlon's gut as he heard the words he'd forgotten twenty-five years ago. His friend, his best friend, hands trembling on the rifle as he tried to do what she asked of him. Tried to please his mama—

"Oh, Jamie."

"She said it was the only way. With Jasper gone and the family jockeying for control, it was the only way to secure my place in the peckin' order." Bitterness edged Jamie's voice. "I was a good son, wasn't I? That's what she told me."

"You never wanted this."

"Yeah, well, I got it now, don't I?"

"You didn't want to kill him." Scanlon meant the words as a statement of fact, but there was still just enough doubt left inside him, doubt about his memories, that it sounded more like a question.

Jamie stopped and stood in front of the door, his chin up as if he'd made a decision. "No, I did not. I didn't want to do any of it. Not then." He closed his hand around the doorknob and opened the door. "And not now."

To Scanlon's surprise, Jamie walked out the door and closed it behind him, leaving Scanlon alone in the parlor. There was a rattle of keys in the dead bolt—locking him in?—and footsteps retreating across the porch steps before they went silent.

Maybe it was a trick. Some sort of trap. But Scanlon couldn't afford to waste the chance to free himself.

He'd been working at the duct tape on his right hand while Jamie paced, loosening it enough that he was able to pull his hand free. He retrieved the penknife from the hidden pouch in his waistband and cut the rest of his restraints free.

He tried the doorknob and found it turned uselessly in his hand. The dead bolt was locked.

He went through the house to the back and found the back door also locked. Worse, the backyard was fenced in, and three large pit bull mix dogs paced the yard, looking mean and hungry.

The front it is, he thought, hurrying back to the front parlor. But as he started to test one of the front windows, movement in the yard outside caught his eye.

It was Opal, returning. And she wasn't alone.

Walking along a step behind her was Isabel, dressed in a camouflage jacket, olive-drab jeans and a pair of hiking boots. Her dark hair was pulled back in a ponytail, and her wary gaze was pinned to the back of Opal Butler's head.

She knows, he realized. *She knows who Opal is. She may even know I'm waiting here inside.*

Which meant she probably had a plan. And as much as he wanted to charge out there right this very moment and make Opal Butler pay for what she forced her young son to do, he wasn't going to put Isabel in greater danger to do it.

She thought he was a captive. So did Opal.

So he sat back down in the chair, wrapped the torn duct tape loosely around his ankles, tucked his hands behind his back and settled down to wait for his partner's next move.

He heard footsteps on the porch. A rattle of the doorknob and a soft sound of surprise from Opal's lips. After a couple of seconds, he heard a key slide into the lock and set himself for whatever came next.

The door opened, and it was Isabel who appeared in the doorway, smiling back at Opal as she entered. "Thanks for the offer of something to drink," she said. "It's hotter out there than I anticipated."

The second she cleared the door, Isabel whipped to the side, putting the door between her and Opal, catching the woman off guard. Opal started to back-pedal, calling out, "Jamie!"

Scanlon pushed from his chair and lunged for her, surprised to find she was quicker than her age would have suggested. Before he reached her, she had pulled a long-bladed knife from the pocket of her jeans and slashed it at him, nearly catching him in the neck.

He stumbled back, and Opal started running down the steps and out into the woods, her steps fast and sure.

"Tell me you're armed," Scanlon growled, as Isabel ran to his side.

She handed him her Beretta and pulled the Smith & Wesson .38 from her ankle holster, following him out into the woods.

They hadn't made it a hundred yards before a rifle shot cracked through the woods, stirring birds into flight from their perches in the trees overhead.

Ahead, Opal Butler's legs churned twice more in the underbrush, then she pitched forward onto her face.

Scanlon and Isabel both hit the ground. "Where did that come from?" Isabel asked.

Scanlon peered toward a ridge above the house, which lay in a shallow hamlet in the mountain. At the top of the ridge, moving among the trees, he saw a male figure silhouetted against the watery afternoon sun. He stood for a long moment, as if gazing down on the scene, then walked away, out of sight over the ridge.

Jamie, Scanlon thought, his gaze moving back to Opal Butler's prone figure. He watched for any sign of movement, but she was deathly still.

After a couple minutes more passed without further movement from Opal, Scanlon looked at Isabel. "Watch my back."

Her dark eyes glowed with a promise that sent warmth rushing into his chest. "Always."

Opal was dead. She'd probably died before her

legs had stopped churning, the shot perfectly positioned through her heart. Just like his father.

"Eye for an eye," he murmured.

"Who was that?" Isabel gazed toward the ridge.

"I'll tell you everything as soon as we get the hell out of this place," he answered, grabbing her hand and heading down the mountain as fast as his shaking legs would take him.

BY THE TIME THEY REACHED the old barn, the area was swarming with FBI agents and Coopers. A relative-filled reunion with her family was cut short when Huntsville resident agents whisked her and Scanlon away for debriefing.

It was two hours later before she got even a glance at Scanlon, across the FBI office. Three hours before they were finally released and she managed to sneak away from her worried family to track him down in an empty office, where he sat at a desk with his head in his hands.

"No charges against Dahlia," she told him, sitting in the empty chair across from him. "Too hard to prove she was up to anything actionable, so nobody wants to try."

"Maybe she'll keep her nose clean now." Scanlon didn't sound convinced.

"Nobody's been able to find Jamie Butler," she added.

He looked up at her. "He probably knows a dozen ways to melt into those hills. Look how long it took the FBI to find Eric Robert Rudolph when he went to ground."

"I hear Jamie as much as confessed to killing your father." She eyed him warily, not sure what he was thinking at the moment. Given how long he'd been chasing his father's nameless, faceless killer, she didn't think he'd just hang up his boots now, when he had a name and a face.

But the clear-eyed look he gave her caught her by surprise. "The woman who killed my father is dead. She made her son shoot a man in cold blood. Jamie was crying and begging not to do it, but she wouldn't give up."

"So we let him off free? He's still a serial bomber."

"I could tell what he's been doing all these years has been eating him up. I think sooner or later, he'll either turn himself in or end it himself. That's up to him."

"I gave Jesse the key," she said. "He's out looking for the lock it belongs to right now."

"Maybe he'll find it." Scanlon didn't sound that interested as he pushed to his feet and walked around to her side of the desk, crouching next to her. He reached up and pushed a lock of hair away from her face, tucking it back into her ponytail. "But I'm done, Cooper. With all of it."

She wasn't sure what he meant, and the way his fingers lingered over her cheek wasn't exactly help-ing her keep her wits. "Done with the case?"

"Done with the FBI." He ran his thumb over her

bottom lip. "Done with anything that keeps me away from you. I love you."

She released a shaky breath. "Oh."

His expression grew uneasy. "That's what you want, too, isn't it?"

She caught his face between her hands. "Of course. I love you, too. Being with you is all I want. But if you want to stay with the FBI, I'll go back. It's not against the rules—"

"I don't want to go back." He pulled her to her feet, wrapping his arms around her. "In fact, I kind of like your earlier idea. Think your brother can find an opening at Cooper Security?" He bent until his lips hovered just above hers.

"He will or I'll kill him," she breathed against his lips.

Chuckling, he slanted his mouth against hers and kissed her, sending joy dancing through her heart.

Epilogue

"It's stupid to wait," Isabel protested. "I'm not sentimental about white dresses and diamond rings—and we've known each other forever—"

"I wish you didn't sound as if you view getting married as something unpleasant to get over with," Scanlon answered, playing with one of the curls spilling onto his shirt.

She rose on her elbow and looked at him. "I don't see it that way. I promise."

"I know your mom walking out didn't give you a good feeling about marriage in general—"

"I want to be married to you," she said firmly, bending to kiss him. He struggled to keep his desire in check, since they weren't exactly alone. Her brothers and sisters had left them alone cuddling on a blanket near the creek in front of Isabel's house, but her yard wasn't large enough to put them completely out of sight.

They were celebrating a happy announcement—Isabel's brother Rick and his wife, Amanda, were having a baby. An impromptu picnic had spilled out of Isabel's pretty little farmhouse onto the back lawn. Only Jesse was missing, though he'd called a while ago to let them know he was on the way.

Sooner or later, Scanlon and Isabel were going to have to drag themselves off the blanket and back into the family fold. But first, he sneaked a quick kiss that damned near derailed his good intentions.

The sound of a car pulling into Isabel's gravel driveway gave Scanlon the strength to pull away. "Is that Jesse?"

Isabel's brow furrowed. "He sounded strange when he called. I wonder if he had any luck in Borland?"

Jesse had found a storage company in nearby Borland that had records of Trey Pritchard renting a small unit. Apparently Trey had paid for ten years' rental up front, so the contents had not yet been auctioned off. Jesse had gone there this morning to meet the manager.

Hand in hand, they crossed to where the rest of the family lounged on blankets and in lawn chairs. Jesse walked up just as they arrived. He held a large manila folder, looking pleased.

"Is that it?" Scanlon asked.

Jesse nodded. "I think your boss is going to be pretty happy with what we found."

Inside were printed photographs of a handwritten ledger detailing years of money laundering through Tolliver Feed and Seed. There were also handwritten notes from Pritchard himself, detailing his growing fear that the Swains intended to kill him.

"It'll be enough for a warrant," Scanlon agreed.

"Maybe it'll give the FBI leverage to get one of the Swains to tell them where Jamie is hiding," Isabel added, looking up at him with shining eyes. "Maybe it can all finally be over."

"Maybe," he agreed. And he'd be glad if it came to pass.

But it wasn't his reason for living anymore.

Isabel was.

She seemed to read his mood, rising to her toes to kiss him. He heard groans from her brothers and sisters at the public display and had the sudden urge to drive up to the Smokies and find the first available wedding chapel.

"Let's elope," Isabel murmured against his lips. "Gatlinburg's pretty this time of year."

Partnership, he thought, smiling through the kiss. He and Cooper had raised it to an art form.

* * * * *